STAMPEDE!

Men in bedrolls awoke too late to get out of the way of the onrushing horses. Remington did enough shouting and shooting to sound like a tribe of Apaches, and it was several seconds before the men realized that it was not.

Some of the outlaws returned fire into the night, wasting their bullets but venting their rage. The rush of horses was gone as quickly as it had come, but it did its damage.

Ramsey Clagg, hand clapped to a bleeding forehead, screamed at the top of his voice: "Goddam you, Remington! I'm gonna kill you slow and hard. *Real* hard!"

REMINGTON #1

WEST OF THE PECOS

JAMES CALDER BOONE

AVON
PUBLISHERS OF BARD, CAMELOT, DISCUS AND FLARE BOOKS

REMINGTON #1: WEST OF THE PECOS is an original publication of Avon Books. This work has never before appeared in book form.

AVON BOOKS
A division of
The Hearst Corporation
105 Madison Avenue
New York, New York 10016

Copyright © 1987 by James Calder Boone
Published by arrangement with the author
Produced in cooperation with Taneycomo Productions, Inc., Branson, Missouri
Library of Congress Catalog Card Number: 87-91116
ISBN: 0-380-75265-4

First Avon Printing: June 1987

AVON TRADEMARK REG. U.S. PAT. OFF. AND IN OTHER COUNTRIES, MARCA REGISTRADA, HECHO EN U.S.A.

Printed in the U.S.A.

K-R 10 9 8 7 6 5 4 3 2 1

WEST OF THE PECOS

Chapter One

Judge Samuel Parkhurst Barnstall ran an informal court. Although the stocky man possessed a law degree from Harvard University, this was Stone County, Missouri, not Boston, Massachusetts, and different rules applied.

For one thing, Judge Barnstall was quite fond of delivering little lectures. He was well aware that in the end, it was the punishment he meted out that set the example, that let people know he stood for law and order and nothing else. But he felt that his lectures served a valid purpose.

It was becoming a regular occurrence now for reporters from St. Louis, Springfield, and St. Joe to visit his court. It did not seem to matter whether there was a controversial case or just some routine sentencings for minor offenses.

What these newspapermen were interested in was justice, the type of swift, sure justice that Samuel P. Barnstall stood for. Besides presiding over trials and sentencing those convicted, part of his job was deterrence, too.

Governor Benjamin Gratz Brown had made that aspect of the job perfectly clear when he appointed him. No more would lawbreakers think the court still operated the way it had under Judge Lucius Binder, Barnstall's predecessor. Binder could be bought and sold as easily as a cheap whore. Not Sam Barnstall. He was a different kind of man. He was out to make this back door to the West a safe place for decent folks to live, and he would stretch the law as much as he had to to do it.

Barnstall scanned the document the court clerk had just handed him. The judge was not a big man, but seated behind

1

his high wooden bench he seemed like a giant, especially to the quivering men who stood before him for sentencing.

The most amazing feature about him was his piercing blue eyes. Criminals who looked into them knew that their fun was over, that they had come to the end of the line and there would be no escaping this man's wrath. They knew that he represented the harsh legal retribution of the weak and helpless who had been wronged.

Barnstall glanced out at the courtroom audience, then cleared his throat.

"The prisoner will rise."

Harvey Harris, a hulking oaf of a man, slowly pulled himself to his feet. Harris's court-appointed defense lawyer, Gideon Ford, stood with him behind the small oak table.

"Mr. Harris, you have been tried and duly convicted of the crimes of kidnapping and rape. Yours was a particularly ugly crime. Not only did you abduct a young woman from her father's farm, but you terrorized her just for the sadistic sport of it, then you forced your filthy self on her. Until you violated this girl, she was a virgin.

"These offenses in themselves are heinous enough and cry out for punishment. But in this case they were doubly compounded by the fact that the young woman you attacked was slow-minded and, although eighteen years of age, has the intelligence only of an eight-year-old child." Barnstall spoke slowly, to make sure that the prisoner understood—and that the reporters had time to write down every word. Then he continued.

"Mr. Harris, there are some who believe that people like your unfortunate victim are not worthy of the same rights as the rest of us citizens. If anybody in my jurisdiction believes that, they'll find out today that they are wrong.

"So, Mr. Harris, your luck has run out. The people of Missouri are outraged by the way you have lived your life.

"And I am outraged that you could commit such an act and think you could, at the most, get away with jail time. For these crimes of kidnap and rape, I hereby sentence you to hang by the neck until dead."

Harris's dulled eyes nearly jumped out of his head. His heavy jaw opened to protest, but no words came.

"Your Honor, this is most irregular!" shouted Gideon Ford. "The death penalty for rape? Surely, Your Honor—"

"Surely I've had a gutful of Mr. Harris and his kind, Mr. Ford," Barnstall barked back. "That poor girl will carry the mental scars of this atrocity for the rest of her life. By God, we're going to have order in this part of the country, even if it means sending each and every Harvey Harris to the gallows. As for the penalty I've imposed, Mr. Ford, if you'll review your statute books, you'll see that it's well within the law."

"But, Judge . . ." the lawyer pleaded.

"Do you want to try for contempt, Mr. Ford? Bailiff, remand Mr. Harris into custody. His execution will be at seven tomorrow morning. The state doesn't want to have to pay for his meals and lodging any longer than it has to."

Two burly guards led the manacled man out of a side door of the courtroom, toward the jail cells below. After a pause, Barnstall turned and looked at his court clerk, standing behind and to the left. The man shrugged and said, "That's all on the docket for today, Your Honor."

"Good. In that case, court is adjourned until nine tomorrow morning." He smacked the walnut gavel soundly on the bench.

"All rise," intoned the clerk.

As Barnstall stood he noticed a tall man sitting in a back row of the courtroom. They made brief eye contact, and the judge gave him a barely perceptible wink. But there was no humor in the action; it was a sign of recognition, a signal that they were both members of a common team, fighting the same dangerous enemy. The judge gave a slight tilting of his head before he opened the hallway door leading to his chambers.

Chief Territorial Marshal Ned Remington moved his lanky frame off the hard wooden bench at the back of the room and exited by the courtroom door. Out in the hall, he slapped his Stetson back on his head again.

Remington was a tall, lean man, with not an ounce of fat on his body. He had black hair, just curling over his ears, and the type of beard that a man can shave at sunup and need to shave again by noon. His eyes were as gray as gunmetal, but sometimes they had a bit of sparkle, when he was especially pleased with himself.

He walked with the ease of a big mountain cat, carrying himself with the confidence of a man sure of his abilities.

Ned Remington had to be sure of himself. He was the man who carried out Judge Samuel Parkhurst Barnstall's orders, the man in charge of rounding up outlaws from the far corners of the Nations so they could suffer Barnstall's justice.

The nod meant the judge wanted to see him in his chambers. And Remington had a notion it would involve more than just congratulations for bringing in Harvey Harris.

The marshal gave a sharp rap on Barnstall's door.

"Come in," came a muffled reply from inside.

Remington entered the judge's chambers. The office was small but neat, as ordered and organized as the jurist's sharp mind. The walls were of a polished walnut paneling, but little of it showed because they were lined with bookshelf after bookshelf. Most of them contained lawbooks and legal treatises, though there were several rows on American history and the Founding Fathers. Maps on the wall showed the western United States and the Indian Nations. Beside Barnstall's framed Harvard law degree was a plaque inscribed *Ignorantia legis neminem excusat*—Ignorance of the law is no excuse.

"Have a seat, Ned," the judge said. There was a weariness in his voice. The old Seth Thomas showed quarter after five, and Barnstall had been at it since early morning.

Remington eased himself into a leather-covered chair opposite the desk. Barnstall got up, went to a mahogany liquor cabinet, brought out a bottle of bourbon and two lead-crystal shot glasses.

"I'll be glad when that scum Harvey Harris makes the drop," Barnstall commented as he poured the amber liquid.

"He's the worst, all right," Remington agreed. "But don't you think you were pushing it just a bit with the death sentence? You can't hand that out to everybody, you know."

"As you said, Ned, he's the worst, and the worst deserve

the worst. Besides, the courtroom is my responsibility. Your job is just to get them here."

Remington took the drink and set it down on a cork coaster. "I have a feeling there's another one we *just* have to get here."

Barnstall's face was grim. He reached in a desk drawer and pulled out a stack of parchment arrest warrants.

"We've got a bad one this time, Ned."

"They're all bad, Your Honor, or you wouldn't be concerned with them. Gimme the details."

"Fella named Ramsey Clagg," Barnstall replied, reading from the warrant.

"I've heard of him. Buffalo hunter. Petty brawler, drunk. Knife fighter. He's just an overgrown kid."

"Huh-uh. He's graduated now, Ned. He killed a lawman out west of here."

Remington picked up his glass and tossed back the whiskey. It was an unwritten law that they all obeyed: Whoever harmed a lawman was an enemy to all of them.

"What happened?"

"Victim's name was Pete Trask, a sheriff's deputy in a little town named Cable, just south of Wichita," the judge paraphrased from a report. "Clagg broke another man's arm in a barroom fight and Trask was tracking him. Apparently Clagg got the drop on him, knocked him out, cuffed him with his own manacles, then hung him upside down from a tree. Clagg tore off Trask's shirt and made some cuts on his body, thinking the deputy would bleed to death. The witness who found Trask's body said it looked like the wolves and coyotes finished him off."

"Hell of a way to go."

"I don't want Mr. Clagg afforded the same courtesy. I want him back here, in my court, so I can watch the son of a bitch's face turn blue when they drop the trap on him. I want him alive, you understand, Ned?"

"Just Clagg?"

"He'd be enough to handle by himself, but word is he might have a couple lowlifes with him. One's named Jake Virgil and the other goes by Snuff Tully. The three of them robbed a bank in Texas about a month ago, but Lord knows whether they're still together or not. When Pete Trask got strung up, Clagg was the only one seen around Cable. Here are the arrest warrants on all three, along with some wanted posters out of Texas that have drawings of their faces and descriptions."

Remington looked the papers over in silence, his face as emotionless as a granite cliff. Finally he got up and went to the door.

"Remember, Ned, these men are all killers. I want them brought back to my court to stand trial."

The marshal turned. "Yeah. I'm the only man for this job."

Remington returned to his own office. It was a simple stone-and-wood building up the street from the courthouse. In the front were a desk and table and a couple of battered chairs, a potbellied stove, and a cot where he slept. On the wall was a rack with a half-dozen Henry repeating rifles and double-barreled shotguns. A few small cells were at the rear of the building.

He dug a lucifer from his vest pocket, popped it on his thumbnail, and touched it to the wick of a kerosene lamp.

Sitting down at his desk, he reviewed the papers the judge had given him, then consulted his own map of the Indian Nations. The little town of Cable was a distance away, a good couple days' ride at least.

The bank these men had hit was in southern Texas. They had covered a lot of territory, managing to elude the Lone Star State authorities along the way. That meant they had to have more than a little cunning.

Sometimes the size of the area he covered overwhelmed Marshal Remington. This country was so huge, and there were so few men to police it. Oh, the local lawmen did their best to maintain peace and prevent range wars, but they did not have the manpower or the time to go chasing all over the Nations for these hardened criminals.

That was where Barnstall, Remington, and his men came in. Governor Brown was determined to stop the lawlessness that had flourished under Lucius Binder. Remington and his deputies had broad powers. They could cross state lines, work without written warrants, search and seize at will. They were backed by the power of the United States government, but once out on the range, their authority came from their Colts and their Henry rifles.

Barnstall was not concerned with methods, but he did issue one irrevocable edict: *If any U.S. marshal or deputy breaks any state or federal laws while in the service of the court, he shall be tried and sentenced for any crime or crimes committed while under the court's jurisdiction.*

Remington had been a U.S. marshal for years before Judge Barnstall arrived. He had watched his arrests go sour before the bench of Lucius Binder. He had continued to do his job, though. Finally his complaints—or more likely those of the people—had reached Governor Brown, and he had had the sand to do something about it.

Now when Remington or his men brought a prisoner in, they could be assured that the man would not go free. It made being a lawman feel worthwhile again.

Remington's thoughts were interrupted when the door opened and a bearded old man shuffled in. Gus Ketchum had been a telegraph operator during the War between the States, and now he intercepted and sent wires from the little office in Galena.

The light streaming through Ketchum's green visor made his face look even older than it was. He waved a piece of pulpy tablet paper toward the marshal.

"Got a reply to your wire."

"That came pretty fast," Remington commented. "I just sent it a few hours ago."

"Guess service is improvin' west of here, Marshal. Here."

Remington tried to decipher the old man's scrawls. "Sorry, Gus, but I can't make hide nor hair of your chicken scratchings. How about reading this for me?"

"When the message is comin' in and I'm transcribin' away, I *do* tend to get a mite sloppy," Ketchum admitted. He pulled out a pair of wire-rims, stuck them on his nose, and squinted at the message. "It's from the sheriff in Cable. He says Ramsey Clagg ain't been seen in his parts since his deputy was killed. He doesn't know anything about no Virgil or Tully."

"Is that it?"

"That's all from him. No reply yet on your wires to Wichita and Amarillo."

"Okay. Thanks, Gus. Let me know as soon as they come in, huh?"

"Sure, Marshal." The old man turned and shuffled out. He did not like to leave his key alone for too long. He even slept next to it.

Considering the way Clagg, Virgil, and Tully had moved since they had hit the Texas bank, they could be in Colorado or even Wyoming by now, Remington thought. He would wait until he heard from the authorities at Wichita and Amarillo. Likely they would send wires to all of the small towns around them, wait for the replies to come in, then get back to Remington. He made good use of the telegraph system, limited and unreliable as it was. It could save days on the trail and dozens of dead ends.

The marshal pulled out his pocket watch, popped open the cover, and saw that it was almost nine. He wasn't going to get anything else done at this hour, and the work ahead required all the energy Remington had.

Chapter Two

Remington's horse, a black gelding that he called Shadow, was accustomed to long days and hard nights on the trail. They were a pair well suited to each other.

Both of them could be quiet, sullen; then, for no particular reason, something might strike them funny. To the horse, it was the opportunity to nip his master's butt whenever he saw him bending over. Remington's sense of humor was more subtle, refined to the point where most men thought he had none at all.

Sometimes, like this morning, still an hour before dawn, riding through the hills, the spirited horse beneath him, Ned Remington would allow himself a smile, or even a laugh. Then the horse would shake its shaggy head and run even faster.

Galena's stage road would take him out of town, past a dozen little villages on the way. If he were lucky, he would be able to make Joplin that night.

The marshal could have picked up the train at Springfield, ridden it west to Wichita, then hired himself a horse to go out to Cable. But he liked it this way. On the way back, he would put himself and Shadow on the train to give the mount a rest.

He knew that he would be coming back. It was not arrogance on his part. It was simply a burning self-confidence that his gun hand was faster than any other man's.

Remington was aware that his success as a marshal was due to a never-say-die and never-let-the-other-guy-get-the-upper-hand attitude. This new assignment would test his abilities to the limit.

The miles rolled by as Shadow slowed to a trot and found his rhythm. The sun sneaked over the Ozark Hills to Remington's back, turning the morning sky a pinkish orange. A magpie gave him hell from its perch at the top of a hickory. Remington didn't blame him. It was too early even for birds to be stirring.

It was dark again by the time Remington crossed the Turkey River and passed into Joplin.

Even though it was not as big as Independence or St. Joseph, it was still a good-sized town, several times larger than the backwoods burg of Galena, where Judge Barnstall chose to hold court. Remington suspected that a few wagon trains still pushed west from here, though not as many as in the old days. Settlers were still pouring into the frontier.

He needed a stable and a hotel room and found a place called the Joplin Palace, though the name was considerably more elegant than the building. It was a redbrick affair, two stories tall, with a wooden balcony on the second floor. Its most alluring feature was that it was far from the taverns and gambling houses and would probably afford a good night's rest.

Remington was dressed in dark pants, black canvas jacket, and had the U.S. marshal's silver badge pinned on the left side of his gray shirt. When he walked into the lobby, he had his saddlebags slung over one shoulder, the Henry rifle in his left hand, and his Colt snug in its holster. A portly old gent puffing a pipe sat in an overstuffed chair, straining at a newspaper.

The man at the night desk was pale, gaunt, looking more like an undertaker than a hotel clerk. His eyes narrowed at Remington until he noticed the glint of the badge.

"Man get a decent night's sleep here?" the marshal inquired.

"If that's what he's looking for."

"And if he's looking for something else?"

"Then he'd have to go to one of the other hotels. The Joplin Palace specializes in soft beds and quiet rooms, Marshal. Now, if you've a mind to . . ."

"Huh-uh," Remington said as he dipped the pen in the ink

bottle. "Tonight I need sleep. Did a lot of riding today. Got more to do tomorrow. This might be the last decent night's sleep I get for a spell."

"Room's a dollar a night, in advance," the desk clerk said.

Remington flipped the cartwheel on the counter and started toward the stairs.

"You want the morning clerk to wake you up at dawn, Mr. . . . uh, Remington?"

"I'll be ten miles down the road by then," the marshal said, not turning around.

The room was decent enough, clean. There was a double bed, a stand with a pitcher and a bowl on it, and a single ladderback chair. Remington left the long gun and his saddlebags, locked the door, then went to a saloon up the street to get something to eat.

His purchase of a beer entitled him to raid the free lunch counter. He assumed that the restaurants would be closed at this hour of the night, anyway. The ham sandwich and boiled egg were gratis, but a slice of apple pie cost him a dime. It was worth it.

Remington headed right back to his room after his meal. No sense making friends or enemies in this unfamiliar town. He knew that a marshal's badge could attract bullets the way honey drew a bear. But Remington had never been a man to hide.

Joplin was just a faded memory by the time the marshal rode into Cable, Kansas. It seemed an unlikely place for Ramsey Clagg to have visited.

Shadow's hooves kicked up tiny clouds of dust as Remington walked the horse down the main street. Cable was nothing out of the ordinary, except that there was a sort of pleasantness about the place that almost made the marshal suspicious.

It was a Saturday, or at least Remington thought it was. Children played at the edges of the street, barefoot boys in knee pants and little girls in calico jumpers. Remington wondered if any of those young'uns had belonged to Deputy Pete Trask.

He swung down at the general store, tying his horse to the

bleached-out rail in front. As he had suspected, he drew some odd looks when he walked inside.

Saturday was a day for farmers to venture into town to do their shopping and business. The women in the general store appeared to be of that stock, with red scrubbed faces and muscular arms from doing laundry on a washboard and churning butter.

Remington purchased a box of cartridges for his Colt and a box for the Henry. The store clerk, a white-bearded fellow in vest, white shirt, and sleeve garters, conducted the transaction quietly, saying no more than he had to.

It was odd. For a farm community, he had expected a warmer reception. These were good, decent, upright folk. What did they have to fear from a U.S. marshal?

"Can you tell me where I can find the town sheriff's office?" he asked.

"Cable ain't that big of a town, marshal," the storekeeper replied. "Ride down to the end of Front Street here, and you'll find it on your right-hand side."

"Obliged."

He tipped the brim of his hat to the women and saw them regarding him with a strange emotion in their eyes. He guessed what it was but hoped he was wrong.

When he reached the sheriff's office, he felt a little ridiculous. It was less than a block down from the store. It would have been easier to walk it.

The building reminded him of his own office, though smaller. It, too, was composed of stone and sturdy timbers. He opened the screen door and stepped inside.

"Sheriff? Name's Ned Remington. Chief territorial marshal out of Stone County, Missouri."

"The *hell* you say! You one of Judge Barnstall's boys?" the sheriff asked as he returned Remington's handshake in a strong grip.

The first thing Remington noticed about the sheriff was that the man wore a gold wedding band on his right hand. That might explain why he had not gone after Ramsey Clagg. Or it might not. He was probably in his early forties, with hair that had once been sandy now turning gray. He wore a little

short-barreled Colt's Storekeeper's model that had been con-
verted to metal cartridge, all right close up but worthless at
more than thirty feet. The single impression that Remington
got of him was that the man had not put down any *real* trouble
in a good many years.

"My name's Ben Simmons."

"Guess you know why I'm here, Sheriff."

"You're after Ramsey Clagg. Got your wire a couple days
ago. I wired back, told you I haven't seen Clagg in Cable
since Trask's murder."

"That doesn't surprise me. He'd be stupid to come back
here after killing your deputy. And one thing about Ramsey
Clagg—he's not stupid."

Some red came to the sheriff's cheeks. Remington knew he
had touched a sore spot. He imagined that Ben Simmons
feared the buffalo hunter more than he wanted to let on.

It would do no good to push it. Remington had come here
to do a job, and berating this man would not help him get it
done.

"I sent some wires south of here, into Oklahoma country,
just after Pete . . . anyhow, none of the lawmen down there
had seen Clagg either."

"That doesn't mean much," Remington observed. "Could
be he's steering clear of towns for a while. A man like Clagg
is used to living off the land. The only reason he'd venture
into civilization is for liquor or cards or a woman."

"Well, we've got liquor and cards here in Cable. Saloon
called the Cottonwood. But we don't have any loose women
in town. Decent folks won't allow it. Clagg got drunk up at
the Cottonwood, got into a fight with a local fella name of Eli
Page. Page's kind of a mouthy sort, but he really doesn't
mean any harm. It got out of hand, and by the time Pete got
down there, Clagg had busted Page's arm, then hightailed it
off on that big brown stallion of his."

"Where were you at the time?" Remington had to inquire.

"I was out at a farm a few miles west of town. A pack of
wild dogs was killing chickens, and I was trying to track them
down and shoot them. By the time I got back, Pete had al-

ready left. He put a note on my desk explaining where he went. I guess he underestimated Clagg."

A tightness came to the sheriff's face and he cleared his throat two or three times. Remington saw moistness welling up in Simmons's eyes, but he fought it back.

"He's a wily bastard, all right. You question the people in the saloon about how the buff'ler was armed?"

"A witness said he carried two Colt's Walkers, still percussion. Had a long gun on his saddle, likely a Sharps."

Remington nodded in silence. If Clagg relied on cap-and-ball revolvers as his belt guns, he was not as smart as they said. Those guns were notoriously unreliable, from bad caps or caked powder. But on the other side, if he was any good at all with his left-hand gun, that was something to reckon with.

"I'll be heading out on the trail after Clagg," Remington said. "Mind if I ask a few questions around town here first?"

"Talk to anybody you like, Marshal. Oh, I've got something here might help you." He reached in a desk drawer and brought out a piece of folded brown paper. "It's a map of Kansas, Indian Territory, and Texas. It . . . it was Pete's. I'd like you to have it."

Remington touched the brim of his hat as he tucked the paper in an inside jacket pocket. "Thanks."

"Marshal . . ."

Remington paused at the door.

"Good hunting. I hope you get the son of a bitch."

As he strode down the boardwalk toward the Cottonwood, Remington considered Ben Simmons. It was a strange thing. The sheriff's courage had turned to rust from disuse.

Remington did not intend to ever let that happen to him.

The Cottonwood was more elaborate than the Rusty Bucket back in Galena. Remington suspected that most of the farmers in these parts were churchgoing folk who did their drinking at home and worked too hard for their money to squander it at a poker table. At the bar were a couple of cowboys, nursing beers. A lone man in a green coat, maybe a gambler passing through, sat at a back table by himself, absently shuffling a deck of cards.

The bartender was a tall, gangly sort, with a white close-cropped head of hair and a jumping Adam's apple. Remington figured him to be a European, but he wouldn't be able to place the nationality until he heard him talk.

"Name's Remington. I'm a U.S. marshal, looking for the man that killed Pete Trask."

"Murdering svine. I hope you git him."

Scandinavian. Remington couldn't make it any closer than that.

"You see the fight between Clagg and Eli Page?"

"Yah, I see it, all right. This Clagg, he's one mean fella, for sure. Snapped that Page's arm just like dry kindling."

"Clagg had a pair of Walker Colts. You see a belt knife on him?"

The bartender pulled his chin with one hand while he tried to recall. Remington could almost see the man reconstructing the scene in his mind.

"Yah, vhat you call the skinning knife, eh?"

"In a sheath near his backside."

"Yah."

"This Clagg. How did he move?"

"Fast. He vas a big man. Taller than me and tvice as heavy, but he vas fast in a fight."

"Anything else?"

The barman thought a moment. "Not so good vith his left. This Page, he got in a few good punches. Clagg tried to block them vith his left arm, but he vas too slow."

Remington nodded in appreciation. That was what he wanted to hear. It would mean that the big buffalo hunter was not a true two-gun man, like Hickok or some of the others.

"I appreciate your help."

"Yah. Then you show it by blowing this Clagg's damn head off. Vhat he did to Pete Trask! No man should be allowed to live after such a crime!"

"Don't worry. Clagg'll get what's coming to him."

Remington walked out into the sunlight again and made his way across town to the stable. There was only one stable, just as there was only one store and one saloon. It was the kind of town that had only one of everything.

Even just one lawman, now.

The stablehand was a gawky, woolly-haired teenager who introduced himself as Joey Meeker. He seemed impressed by the U.S. marshal's badge.

"I'm after Ramsey Clagg," Remington told him. "Did you take care of his horse here?"

"Sure did, Marshal. It was sorta weird. Like a cross between a draft horse and an Appaloosa. One of the biggest animals I ever seen—for ridin', that is."

"Ate a lot, did it?"

"Heck, it ate more oats and timothy than a pair of them quarter horses there."

"Think it was fast?"

"It sure was! I seen Clagg come into town on it, and he was goin' at a full gallop. It'd take a pretty strong animal to carry him that fast for very long."

"Good wind."

"Yeah. He was broad across the barrel, but he had heavy haunches, too. I don't know where Clagg got that horse, Marshal, but it was just about the perfect animal for a man his size."

"This is going to help me catch him," Remington said, tossing the boy a dime.

"Really? Jeez, thanks, Marshal. I got just one piece of advice for you. Just make sure you stay on his trail and don't let him get on yours. That stallion of his could run *anything* to the ground."

Remington was beginning to put it together. A piece here, a piece there, answers that a good hunter needed to know about his quarry.

The marshal was ready to get out on the trail, but he reconsidered. He had been pushing Shadow hard the last few days, harder than he wanted to. If he caught Clagg's track, he might need all the endurance the gelding could give him.

On a hunch, the lawman decided to spend the night in Cable.

"Joey, you see that black gelding tied in front of the sheriff's office? I want you to put him up for the night, feed him good, curry him down." He glanced up at the price board and put another quarter, then another dime, in the boy's hand.

Joey Meeker ran off across the dusty street to fetch the marshal's horse.

Remington figured he had learned about all he was going to about this man who called himself Ramsey Clagg. He had picked up some priceless information.

Everything he knew gave him more of an edge. By the time he caught up with his quarry, Remington would almost be able to read his mind.

Remington retrieved his Henry and his saddlebags and found the only accommodations for travelers in Cable, a white clapboard house owned by a widow named Mrs. Kent. She took in roomers on occasion, but Remington wondered how she made a profit of it by charging just fifty cents a night.

Mrs. Kent was a jolly enough sort. When he revealed that he was staying overnight before setting out after Ramsey Clagg, she acted as if Remington were an avenging angel from God.

That struck him funny.

Only the two of them sat down to supper, but there seemed to be enough food for half the town. When Remington tasted the chicken and dumplings, he reminded himself to leave another dollar under his pillow in the morning before he left.

"You've come a long way after that Clagg, Mr. Remington."

"Yes, ma'am. From Stone County, Missouri."

"Gracious! That *is* far. Do you have any idea where he might have gone?"

"I figure south, though I don't have any hard reason for thinking so."

"My guess is that he'd swing north."

"Yeah? Why would you say that, Mrs. Kent?"

"Just an old woman's notion. He's a buffalo hunter, isn't he? I would think that he'd move back north, away from people and cities, try to go up where the herds are, maybe keep from the law for a few months. He might even hire on with a buffalo-hunting crew. Nobody's apt to bother him there."

Remington looked up from his plate. It made damn good sense. He just hoped the woman was wrong.

After peach cobbler, the old woman cleared the table and

dipped water from a copper boiler into the enameled pan to do the dishes.

"That was a mighty fine supper, Mrs. Kent."

"I'm glad you enjoyed it."

"I'm going out for a while now. I may be back late."

"Well, the back door will be open. You know where your room is. The bed will be turned down. What time will you be leaving in the morning?"

"Before dawn, I expect."

"I'll get you a breakfast."

"Oh no, ma'am. No need for that."

"Well, then, you look on the sideboard here before you leave in the morning. There'll be a brown sack for you with biscuits, cold chicken, and some of this cobbler."

Remington started to protest, but she stopped him.

"Go on, now! I won't let it be said that Claramae Kent has ever sent a paying boarder away hungry. You go and enjoy yourself, now, Mr. Remington. And if I don't see you in the morning, good luck, and the Lord ride with you."

"Thank you, ma'am. Thanks for everything."

Sometimes the world baffled Remington. It was hard to believe that there was so much genuine kindness in people like Claramae Kent, and so much downright evil in fellows like Ramsey Clagg.

When the marshal pushed his way through the batwing doors of the Cottonwood, he saw through the smoky haze that the gambler was seated at the poker table and had persuaded three other men to join him. Remington got himself a whiskey and walked over to the open chair.

"Mind if I sit in?"

"Fresh money's always welcome," the man in the green jacket said with a grin. Remington immediately noticed a gold tooth.

As he picked up his cards the marshal inspected the other men. One was the bearded storekeeper he had bought the ammunition from, the second was a cowboy dressed in jeans and chambrays, and the last man was a brown-haired, dirty-looking fellow with a wide-splayed nose and crossed eyes.

Three hands later, Remington's suspicions were confirmed.

The gambler was cheating, but doing it very subtly. He wore a shiny mirrored ring, and as he dealt he could catch the reflections of the bottom sides of the cards. Only the lawman's quick eye detected the move.

Remington decided to have some fun. Whenever it was his turn to deal, he did a bottom-of-the-deck slide that put the right cards in the cowboy's hand.

The gambler, finally spotting the move, knew that his own dishonesty had been detected and began to grow nervous. He started to talk, out of apprehension.

"What brings a U.S. marshal all the way out to a nowhere town like Cable?" he asked.

"Tracking a killer named Ramsey Clagg, and his pals, Jake Virgil and Snuff Tully."

"Know that fella."

"Huh?" Remington looked up at the cross-eyed man, unsure that he was the one who had spoken.

"Know Virgil," the man repeated. "Hunted buff'lo with him up on the Republican River."

"Yeah? How long ago was that?"

"Couple years. Bastard tried to cheat me outa some of my share. Seen him a week ago."

"Where?" Remington demanded.

Then the man clammed up, thinking he might have said too much, that Virgil, wherever he was, might be able to hear him.

"I said, *where?*"

The man looked into Remington's eyes, narrowed on him with all their awful, hypnotic power. Sweat formed on the short man's upper lip.

"Two days southwest a here," he confessed. "Town name a German Flats."

Chapter Three

By the afternoon of the second day out on the trail, Remington was getting anxious to close with the outlaw named Jake Virgil.

Anyone looking at the lawman would never have been able to guess it. He was as calm and unrattled as if he were back home fishing for catfish.

The closest thing that Remington had to nerves was an innate sense of caution. It was rare that he took a chance that he was not sure he could back up. Long ago he had learned that a marshal stays alive by using his head as well as his gun hand.

He had studied Barnstall's warrants and the wanted poster dozens of times, but they afforded him few real clues about Jake Virgil, the man. He knew, for instance, that the dodger said Virgil was considered armed and dangerous.

Hell, what hard case that he was sent after *wasn't?*

He knew, too, from the man at the saloon, a buffalo hunter and drifter named Jack McCall, that Virgil was not especially skilled with a handgun; he preferred his Sharps or a double-barreled sawed-off.

Virgil, according to McCall and the information on the poster, was nowhere near the size of Clagg, but he was still a big, bulky man who moved slowly, yet had a backbreaking bear hug. Hair, brown. Eyes, brown. Usually a scruff of a beard. No identifying marks except large, jug-handle ears.

Remington had memorized the sketch on the poster. If he saw Jake Virgil anywhere, he would recognize him immediately.

For the tenth time that day, he extracted Pete Trask's map from his vest pocket and unfolded it. It was eerie. Every time Remington opened the document, he caught the aroma of the dead man's pipe smoke. It was almost as if Trask were riding with him.

He spotted the shallow river he had just crossed and figured he was closing in on German Flats. It was on the map, yet Remington had never heard of it.

When Shadow topped a rise, Remington stood in the stirrups and saw German Flats spread out in a broad valley below him. It was a sizable town, bigger than Cable, not as big as Joplin.

Wood smoke from the cookstoves filled the air, creating a sort of haze over the settlement. Remington consulted his pocket watch. In an hour or two it would be suppertime.

He was a smart lawman. He liked to have the odds in his favor. If Jake Virgil were down there, what would he be doing? Would he be playing cards? In bed with a woman? Getting ready to eat? Having a beer? Just sitting in a propped-back chair, whittling?

Remington considered waiting until three or four in the morning, when sleep would slow the robber down, but Virgil would be harder to find then. Folks did not relish being rousted awake in the middle of the night, even by a U.S. marshal, and they often would withhold information they might, in a better humor, have released.

Easing back onto the saddle, Remington patted the gelding on the side of the neck, then moved it at a walk down the hill toward German Flats.

He assumed there was a town sheriff or constable in German Flats. He did not see the office as he rode into the edge of town, but he knew it was there.

Remington wondered whether Virgil was alone or whether Clagg and Tully were with him. McCall had not mentioned seeing the others. Maybe they had split up after robbing the bank. As Simmons had said, there was no evidence to show that Virgil and Tully had been in on the killing of Deputy Pete Trask.

Remington dismounted at the first hitchrail he came to.

There would be only three reactions to the questions he would ask: cooperation, sullenness, or downright belligerence.

Being a lawman meant prodding, probing, stirring up things people would just as soon he left be. Ned Remington had gotten used to it a long time ago. Most good folks respected the law and appreciated what he was doing. People who felt guilty or had something to hide always had a hard time disguising it.

The store in front of him was a dress shop. No need inquiring about Virgil there. Next to it was a land office. That would be of no use either.

Up the boardwalk a piece was a café. Remington turned in there and opened the door.

The inside of the establishment was nothing to brag on. There were red-checkered tablecloths, rough pine chairs, a blackboard with the menu written on it, and a wooden counter to the side. Two older fellows dressed in suits—bankers or cattlemen, Remington suspected—sat at a corner table drinking lemonade. Empty plates were pushed to the center.

The cook, a friendly-looking man, came out of the kitchen, wiping his hands on a towel. "What can I get you, Marshal?"

"Glass of that lemonade," Remington said. He was dry from the trail, but he did not want to put any liquor in himself, not even a beer. He downed the tumbler in three big gulps, then handed the man a nickel. "I'm looking for a man who might be in German Flats." He showed the poster of Virgil.

"Yeah, I've seen him, all right," the cook confirmed. "He was in here a couple days ago, but I haven't seen him since. There's another eat place in town. Cheaper, but not as clean as us."

"He have anybody with him?"

"No. Not that I recall. Wish I could help you more."

"You've been more help than most. Either of you two gents seen this man?" Remington showed the poster to the two in the corner. They both shook their heads in silence.

On a hunch, he crossed the street and went down a side street, following his nose. There was a livery stable and, next to it, a large corral. If Clagg were in town, Remington would be able to spot the big stallion immediately. He doubted there were two riding horses like that in this part of the country.

The stablehand had never heard the name Jake Virgil, but he recognized the drawing. He led Remington down a row of stalls and pointed out a shaggy buckskin as Virgil's horse. On the bridle was a small numbered tag. Virgil had been given a wooden tag with the corresponding number that he would turn in when he came back to claim his horse and settle his bill.

"How long has he been here?"

"A week," the man sad, rummaging through a stack of papers on a small table. "Say, he's not gonna try to run out on his bill, is he, Marshal?"

"Not unless he gives me some trouble. I want you to hold this horse, you understand? If Virgil comes back for it, stall him any way you can. Tell him it's been sick and can't be ridden for a day or two."

"Yessir, I'll do 'er."

Remington went back across the street, knowing now that Virgil was somewhere in town. The badge made the marshal a perfect target. If Virgil saw him first, he would know that a U.S. marshal would only be in this town looking for him.

From what Remington had picked up about Jake Virgil, it would be the outlaw's style to backshoot him.

Just last night, Remington had cleaned and lubricated his Colt, replaced the loads with the fresh ammunition he had purchased in Cable. He had checked the primer on every cartridge before he put it in the cylinder, but that did not guarantee that his hammer would not fall on a dud. That fraction of a second before he could cock and pull the trigger again could mean his death.

He hoped it was only his imagination that made him feel as if he were in somebody's rifle sights as he walked across the wide expanse of street to the shelter of the porches over the boardwalk.

At the first saloon he tried, a sedate, respectable establishment, he got no response when he asked, then showed the poster around. So many blank faces convinced him that no one had seen Jake Virgil in there.

The next saloon was a step down, with rancid-smelling

sawdust on the floor instead of polished brass spittoons. The people there were coarse, the girls tired-looking, the bartender defensive.

Most of them shrugged or shook their heads when he showed them the poster. Finally a toothless man trying to gum a sausage sandwich admitted that Virgil had been in there the night before.

"He put away enough beer to kill a normal man," the eater said, wiping his chin with a shirt sleeve.

"You two got to talking any?" Remington asked.

"Naw. I ain't no friend of his, mind yuh. We just had us a few beers together. I couldn't keep up with him. It was near twelve-thirty when I left here, and he was still pourin' 'em down like there was no tomorra."

"Obliged, mister."

As Remington left he made sure not to turn his back to any of them. It could be that the man had been lying about not being a friend of Virgil.

A half hour later he had turned up nothing in German Flats' two hotels. He was almost convinced Virgil had slept off his drunk in an alley, when he saw a faded sign for Burnee's Rooming House—*Day or Week Rates, Cheap.*

It was a two-story frame house with a picket fence that had not been painted since the war, and faded whitewash clapboards that looked more like dried bones than wood.

The yard was overgrown in weeds, grasshoppers bouncing from one to the other. There was a useless swing, hanging by only one chain, on the porch.

Remington loosened his Colt in its holster before he even put his left hand on the doorknob. Virgil might be in the parlor or the dining room.

The darkness inside momentarily threw Remington off guard. He noticed dusty velvet drapes at the front windows, blocking most of the light. After a few moments, his eyes became accustomed to the gloom.

Remington thought to call out for the proprietor, then decided to keep quiet. That might warn Virgil, if he were here.

Hand on his gun, he checked the parlor to the left. Some

rocking chairs, a settee, a piano with yellowed keys. No one there.

A glance inside the dining room to the right told him the same thing. The table was set with heavy stoneware, utensils, and drinking glasses.

Remington slowly moved down the hallway off the dining room. He smelled food cooking and assumed that the kitchen was behind the double doors.

The wooden floor creaked under his bootheels with every step.

He pushed the door open and saw a sweating fat man toiling at a big kettle on the cookstove. The man was about to toss more kindling in the stove when he noticed Remington.

The barely perceptible tightening under the big man's eyes told Remington that he was one of those who would not readily cooperate. That was all right. Remington was sure Jake Virgil was staying here.

"Help you with something, mister?"

He had glanced at the badge but deliberately called him "mister." That told the marshal something about him.

Remington shook out the wanted poster and held it out with his left hand. "Jake Virgil. I'm looking for him. He staying here?"

There was silence. A drop of sweat trickled down the man's forehead and along the side of his nose. He tried to act calm.

"Don't know no Jake Virgil."

The marshal answered without blinking. "I'll ask it one more time. I'm looking for this fella. He robbed a bank down in Texas. Now, you can tell which room he's in, or I can march you up those damn steps, my gun in your back, and make you open up the room ahead of me."

The man's eyes grew wide and white. Remington could practically read his thoughts: *Hell, I don't owe nothing to this Virgil. He's a lousy four-bit-a-night boarder, and I'll probably have to air his room out for a week after he's gone. I think this lawman means it. No, I'm sure he does. He looks just mean enough to do that. I don't owe that bastard Virgil nothing.*

"He's in two-oh-eight. Or could be he's in two-ten."

"You don't *know?*" Remington took a step forward, grabbing the man's shirtfront.

"I swear I don't. His room is two-ten. But I had a widow, travelin' to Denver, was kinda givin' him the eye. She was willin'. I don't know whether Virgil took her up on it or not."

That put a twist to it. Remington did not want any innocent bystanders to be harmed. If Virgil was in with the woman, he could easily use her for a shield.

"Did you see him go by?" Remington demanded.

"Nope. I been in the kitchen here the last hour or two."

"How about the woman? Why would she be in her room during the day?"

"How the hell would I know? Because she's paying for it, maybe? Listen, mister, my boarders come and go as they please. This ain't no damn convent."

The man was regaining his courage. Remington had to stomp on it hard to get control back.

"Okay. Okay. You can just take me for a little tour of the upstairs rooms, starting with two-oh-eight." Remington let his hand slide down to the butt of his Colt.

"No, no. I . . . I got work to do. I got food to get ready."

"It'll wait." The marshal was not going to let him weasel out. "Tell you what, Mr. Burnee. You give me passkeys to those two rooms—and keep your mouth shut—and I'll let you stay down here." Remington's expression was as cold as a January morning.

"They're in the desk in the parlor."

Remington followed the fat man through the doors, down the hall, through the dining room, and into the front room. The desk the man had mentioned was only a high writing table with stacks of ledgers and papers on it.

Burnee slid open the center drawer. Remington's index finger slid into the trigger guard of his forty-four. The fat man might have a gun in that drawer.

The chubby fingers dug around, pushing pencils and pens aside. A drop of perspiration that had collected on the end of Burnee's ball nose finally dripped off, splattering on a rusty letter opener.

"Here they are. My extra keys to two-oh-eight and two-ten."

They were tied to little oval-shaped, flat wooden tags with the numbers written on them in heavy pencil. Remington took them in his left hand.

"I'm going to warn you now, Burnee, and I'm only going to do it once. You keep your mouth shut. You keep from walking around. You don't make any noises. In fact, if I was you, I'd get the hell out of here for the next half hour. If shooting starts, I've got a feeling these walls might not stop too many bullets."

The man made an audible gulping sound, but there was no way his Adam's apple could be seen under a half-dozen chins. He heeded Remington's advice, not even bothering to strip off the soiled apron as he departed by the back door.

That made the marshal feel better. Now he did not have to worry about any shots coming from his back. He had no idea whether Burnee could have been trusted. Having him gone relieved any doubts.

Remington looked at the stairway. It came down into the hall and was narrow. Two people could not fit side by side.

Some light filtered down from the second floor. Remington drew his Colt and cocked it, muffling the noise as much as he could by holding the revolver inside his jacket.

When he stepped on the first board stair, it let out a moaning squeak. He considered taking his boots off, but then he thought that if Virgil escaped out the window and ran, the outlaw could be gone before Remington had time to run down to his boots and put them on. He continued upward.

What to do?

If he tried the widow's room first and she was alone, she might raise such a ruckus that she would wake Virgil up and warn him. If he *was* in that room with her, he was sure to use her as a hostage.

If he tried Virgil's room first and Virgil was in with the widow, they might hear him opening the door. Virgil would be ready for him by the time he found the right room.

Remington felt the hairs on the back of his neck rise.

He decided to try the widow's room first. It was just an

illogical hunch, one of those inner warnings he sometimes listened to.

By keeping to the outsides of the boards, he managed to hold the squeaks from the stairs down to a minimum. He was at the top. Only five doors faced out on the hall: 208 through 212. Remington figured one of the rooms might be Burnee's. He did not think there were any bedrooms downstairs.

As quietly as he could, Remington moved beside the door to 208, the widow's room. Knocking was out of the question.

He stood stock-still, listening.

No sound came back to him.

Standing to the side, Remington gently inserted the key in the lock. It made an excruciatingly loud clanking noise when he turned it. Then he grabbed the knob, twisted it, and pushed in.

A woman in her mid-fifties, dark hair turning to gray, clad in a long dressing gown, leaped out of a wicker chair, her dime novel falling to the floor.

"Who are you? How *dare* you come in here?" she snapped.

"Quiet!" the marshal snarled in a low tone. "I'm looking for a man named Jake Virgil."

There was color in her cheeks now and she wanted to give him a tongue-lashing, but she noticed that he had the gun pointed at her.

"Mr. Virgil is in the room next door," she whispered.

"You saw him go in there?"

"No. But I heard him last night. Made a terrific commotion when he came in, drunk. Woke me and all the other boarders. I could hear some of the others shouting at him. I stayed in here with my door locked."

He took her by the arm and guided her to the open door.

"Ma'am, I want you to get out of here."

"Like this? I'm half dressed. Wait outside while I change."

"No time. Go down and wait in the dining room. There might be shooting."

She looked into the eyes of this stranger but could read no emotion.

"Go. Go."

"Yes," she said, fear suddenly bubbling up in her. "Yes, I'm going."

She breezed past him and went down the steps, creating a symphony of squeaks as she did.

Remington eased down the hall.

He stopped, leaning against the wall beside Virgil's door. Holding his breath, he listened again, sure that the talk with the woman must have awakened the buffalo hunter.

A sound was coming from the room, but Remington could not distinguish it. It might have been snoring.

He inserted the passkey and turned. Again came the metallic banging of the tumblers.

Remington gripped the doorknob with his left hand and turned. The latch slipped out of the plate. The door swung inward on its own weight.

This room was different from the widow's. Though it was evening and the sun was still up, there was no light coming in the window. A shade might have blocked some of it, but it would not have turned the room this black.

As Remington's eyes adjusted he saw that a heavy wool blanket had been hung over the curtain rod. He listened again.

There was heavy breathing. A sort of wheezing. Was it snoring?

This was it. With his left hand, Remington clamped his hat down tight on his head. Still standing in the hallway by the wall, he shouted as loudly as he could.

"Virgil! Jake Virgil! This is the law. I'm arresting you for the bank job in Texas. Come out with your hands up!"

The shotgun blast ripped away a two-foot section of the doorframe, sending vicious splinters into the wall across the way.

As soon as he yelled, Remington had dropped to the floor. If he had stood in the same spot, some of the BBs would have come through the thin wall or some of the wood would have impaled his face and throat.

Lying on the floor, he saw the muzzle flash.

He leveled the Colt and triggered off one round into the blackness, his only target the dancing yellow spot before his eyes.

Virgil was unable to stifle the groan. He was hit.

Remington ducked back out into the hall, knowing that the outlaw had probably seen his muzzle blast.

"Last warning, Virgil. My next shot ends it for you. Toss that scattergun out; then you come out after it, hands on your head."

Some low, muttered cursing, more growls than words, came from the room.

Remington waited. He remembered Barnstall's order: Jake Virgil was to be brought in alive. Remington could wait a while longer. After all, he was not the one with a bullet in him, a lawman waiting outside to finish him off.

"Awright!" came a gargly shout. "Awright, goddammit, you got me."

"First the shotgun. And your Sharps."

"Sum a bitch. Sum-a-bitchin' law."

There was a loud clunk on the wooden floor. In the light streaming in from the hallway, Remington could see the tip of the sawed-off. Then the Sharps clattered out on top of it, its barrel halfway out the door.

The bedsprings squeaked. Then the sound of bare feet clumped across the pine floor. Jake Virgil appeared, hands laced on his head, squinting against the light.

Blood was trickling out of the wound in his right shoulder. It had to be painful, but buffalo hunters were men used to hardship. He tried to give Remington his most scathing look, but when he saw the frigid eyes of the lawman, his jaw started to slack open.

"I've got a question for you, Virgil."

"I'm bleedin', Marshal."

"And you ain't going to quit until I get an answer. Where are Ramsey Clagg and Snuff Tully?"

The man's bottom lip jutted out in defiance.

"Suit yourself, Virgil. Clagg and Tully aren't the ones losing blood. I can wait all night." He kept the pistol trained on the man's chest.

Virgil sensed that it was no idle threat. This man meant what he said.

"Don't know where Clagg is. Split with Tully about a week or so ago in a little place southwest of here called Salt Wells."

"I don't like the sound of that. I think we'll just wait a bit longer."

Virgil surveyed the blood oozing from his shoulder and dripping down on his bare feet. "By God, it's the truth! I swear!"

"How good could the word of a thieving murderer be?"

"I ain't never murdered nobody. You gotta believe me about Tully. *Please.*"

"Keep your hands on your head and march down those stairs. Try anything, and I'll blow the top of your head off."

German Flats' sheriff wore almost the same dumbfounded expression when Remington shoved Virgil into his office. The marshal tossed the poster and warrant on the desk.

"Chief Territorial Marshal Remington, out of Stone County, Missouri. This man's my prisoner. I'm leaving him here in your custody. Get him patched up. And, Sheriff . . . he damn well better be here when I come back for him."

Chapter Four

One down and two to go.

Remington knew that Jake Virgil had been child's play, compared to what Snuff Tully and Ramsey Clagg were going to be.

The marshal had picked up quite a bit about Tully along the way. First, there was the information he had gotten from the wanted poster out of Texas. Tully was in his sixties, though an exact age had not been given. He was only of medium height and build, but that did not deceive Remington. He knew that some old men could be as scrappy as bobcats. Tully's hair was gray, or mostly so, with streaks of white in his beard. Remington had learned that the old man carried a conversion of an 1860 Colt's Army model and sometimes packed a single-shot cap-and-ball derringer. Like his two buffalo-hunting friends, Virgil and Clagg, he probably had a Sharps rifle. Remington was more concerned with the handguns.

Virgil had been talkative enough. It was true, Remington thought, that there was no honor among thieves. In fact, there was even some spite, because the first outlaw had revealed the location of his partner without a great deal of prodding.

The country was unfailing in its sameness. On the gently rolling plains, mile after mile, fields of tall grass rippled spring-green in the wind. Some of it was grazing land, home to the longhorns owned by people brave enough to face the Kiowa and Comanche.

Remington was swinging down toward the Texas Panhandle — at least that was what his map told him. He used the sun and stars to navigate by. And there were penciled scrawlings made on the paper by the dead deputy, Pete Trask, pointing out an occasional landmark. A stand of trees was visible for miles, and on occasion there would be a rocky hill, not yet eroded by the ceaseless winds of time.

Jake Virgil had not been easy. Remington realized that he had come within a whisker of getting his head blown away by that sawed-off. Sometimes that whisker was the only distance that mattered. Still, the marshal did not like cutting it that close. His chance-taking was based on common sense, on knowing a man's reflexes and beating them with his own. It was a game that allowed for no wrong moves.

Remington consulted the map again, although he had all but memorized it. Trask had drawn in a small stream, with a notation that the bed was dry much of the year. Remington tugged back gently on the reins. The big black stopped, snorted, and flicked his tail.

"Water hereabouts, Shadow," the lawman said absently. "You like a nice cool drink? Let's see if we can find it."

A bunch of squawbush stood out like a pointing finger. Remington eased his mount down a rise toward the foliage and saw that some scrubby willows and other bushes traced the banks of the narrow creek, pulling in the precious water it supplied.

He dismounted and led the horse to the edge of the water. It was clear for its being spring, though only about six inches deep. The bottom seemed more gravel than mud. Shadow began drinking eagerly. Remington bent and helped himself, a few feet upstream.

Suddenly the lawman swiveled, whipping his gun out of its holster.

Up the hill, a boy, hardly into his teens, dropped a wooden bucket he had been holding and thrust his hands into the air.

Remington's dark eyes narrowed, surveying the rest of the small ravine. No one else was there.

"Didn't anybody ever tell you it's dangerous sneaking up on a man like that, boy?"

The boy made no reply. His eyes were white with fear, caught between blinking away tears and staring at the muzzle of the outstretched pistol.

"Who are you?" Remington demanded.

"My name's Dudley Yates," he said with a stammer.

"You from around here?"

"Farm . . . about ten miles south."

"What are you doing out here in the middle of nowhere?"

"Me . . . me and my grandpa were going to visit my uncle. I was just getting some water, mister. Honest, I didn't mean no harm."

"Put your hands down." Remington holstered the gun. "C'mon. Get your water, then."

The boy walked slowly down the hill, stumbling once but not falling. Remington noticed that there was something odd about him. He noticed that the boy squinted and occasionally rubbed his eyes.

"You're a U.S. marshal?" he said, looking at the badge.

"Yep," Remington acknowledged. "You got any law in these parts, Dudley?"

"Just old Sheriff Walker." A grin came. "We don't see much of him. Gramps says he spends most of his time hiding." He bent down and filled the bucket in the creek.

"Where is your grandpa?"

"In the wagon, on the other side of the rise."

"Go on ahead, then. I want to talk to him."

Dudley Yates led the way up the hill, still unsteady on his feet. When they reached the top, Remington saw a weathered buckboard below, a pair of snoozing grays harnessed to it. On the seat was an old man dressed in corduroy pants and a loose cotton shirt. A stained, battered cowboy's hat perched on his proud head.

"Gramps's name is Herman. Herman Yates," the boy said, in a half whisper.

Remington walked over to the wagon seat and stuck out his hand. "Name's Ned Remington, Mr. Yates. Chief territorial marshal out of Stone County, Missouri."

The old man stuck his hand out, but he did not reach for Remington's. It was then the marshal understood that Herman Yates was completely blind.

Remington took the old man's hand in a firm grip and shook it.

"Proud to make your acquaintance, Marshal." There was a deep easiness in the voice, an air of command. "I used to be a lawman myself, once."

"Grandpa was a deputy sheriff down in Texas, near the border, weren't you, Gramps?"

"That's right, Dudley. 'Course, that was quite a few years back."

Remington studied the old man's face. He had seen a hundred similar to it, yet none quite like this one. There were the high cheekbones, the long nose, the thin lips, the tanned, leathery skin, the thinning strands of silky white hair. The old man had a ranginess to him that told Remington he must have been quite a hellion in his youth.

"How about a hand down from that wagon, Mr. Yates?"

The lower lip jutted out in defiance—just for a second— then it retracted as the man reached for the steadiness of the other's arm. He gripped the side of the seat, found the rim of the wheel, and lowered himself to the ground.

"You're the first folks I've seen out here for a couple of days," Remington said. "You make this trip often?"

"Not as often as I'd like," replied Herman Yates. "My son, Ed, he can't get away from his ranch as often as he'd like. So Dudley here takes me up to visit my other son, Harvey, every couple of months or so."

"Don't you people have any trouble with the Indians?"

"We've sorta reached an understanding with the Kiowa," the old man said, pulling a plug of tobacco from his shirt pocket. He fished in his pants, brought out a pocketknife, and cut off a chaw. He held the plug out to Remington.

"No, thanks. What do you mean, 'understanding'?"

"We don't have real big spreads. Just enough to live off of. The Kiowa pass by a couple of times a year, we palaver with them for a while, let them cut out a steer for their own use. You might call it . . . cheap insurance."

"Can you trust them?"

Herman Yates stood up taller. "The chief we deal with is an honorable man. We're all honorable men. This really is their land, you know." Then he grinned and gave an unexpected wink. "We're just paying them a little rent."

"Mr. Yates, you've got more sand than most men."

"Yep. Had it all my life. From the time I pinned a star. But tell me, Marshal: What brings you down through these parts?"

"I'm looking for some men who robbed a bank down in Texas. One of them killed a deputy up in a little town called Cable, Kansas."

A clouded expression came over Herman Yates's brow. It told Remington what he had many times suspected: Once a lawman, always a lawman.

"What would these fellas' names be?"

"I've already got one of them in the jail up to German Flats. His name is Jake Virgil. They're all buffalo hunters. The other two are named Snuff Tully and Ramsey Clagg. Clagg's the one with the murder charge on him. You ever heard of them?"

The old man's lips puckered. He pulled a pocket watch out of his pants, popped open the case. The glass had been removed from it so he could feel the numbers and hands with the tips of his fingers.

"Be time for supper in a couple of hours, Marshal. Why don't you camp with us tonight?"

"I don't know . . . I've got a lot of ground to cover. . . ."

"You stay the night with us. I'll tell you all you want to know about Snuff Tully."

Dudley Yates proved to be a surprisingly good cook for a boy of only thirteen. Remington had seconds on bacon and washed down his fourth slice of Dutch-oven bread with a cup of chicory-laced coffee.

"Where'd you learn to cook like that, Dudley?"

"Grandpa taught me, Marshal. I reckon Grandpa taught me just about everything I know. When I get old enough he's gonna teach me how to be a lawman, too."

"Why don't you go get some more wood for the fire before it gets too dark, grandson?"

"Yessir." He ambled off, a small hatchet in one hand.

"He'll never make a lawman," Herman Yates said quietly, once the boy was out of earshot.

"Why's that?"

"He's got it too. It skipped a generation. It skipped his pa and his uncle Harvey, but it got him."

"What?"

"The eye disease. The same one that made me go blind. Oh, the doctors down in Texas had some long, fancy name for it, but they didn't have anything in the way of a cure. God help me, I hope I'm wrong about Dudley."

"Have you taken him to a doctor?"

"We're on the way now. After we stop at Harvey's for a few days, we're going on to Denver. Maybe there's somebody there who can help him."

In the orange glow of the fire, Remington noticed a single tear sliding down the old man's cheek.

"You said you knew Snuff Tully."

Herman Yates cleared his throat, groped for his tin coffee cup, and drank another swallow. "Fill me up there, will you, Marshal?"

He poured the man's coffee and helped himself to some more. "Quite a coincidence I should run into you, Mr. Yates."

"Yep. But not so much about me knowing Tully. It's a big country, Marshal, but not so many people out here yet. Or at least there wasn't when Tully and me were boys."

"You've known him that long? Are you friends?"

The blind man made a face. "We were—once. Maybe thirty, forty years ago, before Tully left home to join the trappers and buffalo hunters. They were a mean bunch. Had to be, to fight off the Indians and the heat and the cold and come out of it alive."

"You didn't go with them?"

"Had no stomach for it," Yates said. "The herds were big in those days. They called them the Brown Sea. Buffalo could run down a valley in front of you from morning till dark and you'd never see the end of them.

"Tully and his kind, they'd just lay up on a hill and blast away all day at a grazing herd. Then they'd go down and skin them, tossing the hides in a wagon and leaving the rest to rot. He was among the first. The Indians were still fierce then, on the warpath against white men, all over the West. But that didn't stop Snuff Tully and his kind. They were getting a top price for buffalo hides, and Tully was out to make as much as he could."

"If that's true, he must have earned a small fortune," Remington ventured.

"Made and lost, Marshal, made and lost. Snuff Tully always had the gambling bug, as long as I've known him. And where there's people with money, there's always others to take it away from them."

"So Tully lost all his hiding money?"

"He bummed around the West for a couple years, trying to get another shooting party together, but couldn't get any takers. When the war broke out, Tully was a natural for Quantrill's raiders."

"Seems a lot of the men we track fell in with him," Remington commented.

"I expect so. Tully might have been a decent man at one time. Hell, buffalo hunting's a rough game, but there's nothing illegal about it. Once he got in with Quantrill, though, I think something inside him sorta went sour, if you know what I mean."

"Yeah. He couldn't leave it behind after the war was over."

"Oh, it wasn't anything serious at first," Yates said, digging out a fresh chaw of tobacco. "Little things, you know, to avoid work. Like stealing a maverick here and there, a couple chickens."

"Sounds like petty stuff to me."

"Tully always had sort of a mean streak in him. Hell, when we went to a one-room schoolhouse on the Arkansas border, he use to beat the stuffing out of half the boys in class."

"But not you."

Yates held his chin high. "I was the only one he was afraid of. Seems like that taste of Quantrill's tactics brought out the worst in him. I'm telling you, Marshal, he crossed the line, and he never went back."

"I have to bring him in—alive," Remington said.

"And you want me to tell you what I can to help you do that."

"That's up to you. I know he was your friend once, but you were a lawman. . . ."

"And Snuff Tully's gone bad, just as sure as a hunk of raw meat left out in the sun. No, what you're asking me isn't betraying any friendship, Marshal. Tully and me quit being friends years ago, when he started riding on the wrong side of the law. How can I help you?"

"How long's it been since you've seen him?" Remington asked.

"A lot of years. Maybe twenty."

Remington thought he might be wasting his time. "Can you tell me anything about the man? You know, something that wouldn't have changed no matter how much time goes by."

Herman Yates thought for a moment, his sightless eyes glazed orange in the glow of the campfire. "He's a patient man. You wouldn't think it, for a rowdy like him, but he's got nerve. He can wait things out. He used to be pretty fast on his feet, but, hell, I was too, thirty-odd years ago. If you get into a fistfight with him, watch his knees. He'll go for your crotch if you give him an opening."

"He use a knife?"

"Don't know. Odds are a buff'ler like him would carry one. He's not a big man, mind you. Doesn't have a lot of power in his hands or arms, but he used to be fairly quick. I expect the years have faded that some."

"What kind of a shot was he—when you knew him?"

"Passable," the old man answered. "Buffalo were a big target, and they weren't moving too much."

"Handgun?"

"Faster'n most. Used to carry his revolver kind of high on his hip, toward the front. Reckon he hasn't changed that much. Like I said, Tully's got nerve. You get in a gunfight with him, he'll take his time, get his gun out, and try to get a good aim on you. No shooting from the hip for him. If you're fast, and accurate, you'll take him, Marshal."

"Judge Barnstall wants him brought back alive."

"Hell!" Yates let out a squirt of tobacco juice that hissed the flames. "You're a lawman. You can't control how he's going to react when you get the drop on him. Your first responsibility is to come out of this alive yourself. World isn't going to mourn a dead bank robber, especially the likes of Snuff Tully."

"Anything else you can tell me? Take your time. Think about it."

The old man sat silent for two, almost three minutes; then he cleared his throat and spoke again. "If I could sum up old Snuff Tully in one word, Marshal, it'd be this: *sneaky.* Yeah, that's it. He'll bushwhack you if you give him a chance. From what I hear lately, he's got no regrets about shooting a man in the back either. If I was you, I sure as hell wouldn't give him an opening."

"I don't intend to," Remington said grimly.

The marshal's gun was in his hand at the sound of a twig snapping just on the edge of camp. Dudley came in, his arms loaded down with deadwood and sticks. He dumped the pile unceremoniously, then let out a noisy sneeze.

"What have you and the marshal been talking about, Gramps? Lawman stuff?"

"Yeah, that's right, Dudley. Lawman stuff," old Herman said. "It's been a long day. You about ready to turn in?"

"Can't I just listen to you and Marshal Remington for a while?" He rubbed at his swollen, watering eyes.

"Your grandpap and me are about through talking," Remington said. "He gave me some mighty useful advice on how to capture old Snuff Tully."

"Is that right, Gramps?"

"Sure. Me and Tully go way back. We were even friends until he became an outlaw."

Dudley went into a minor sneezing spasm, rubbing his eyes again and blowing his nose into a large red handkerchief. After he recovered, he gave a crooked grin to Remington, as if in silent apology for the attack.

"I think I'll spread my bedroll pretty soon, son," said the marshal. "That was a mighty fine supper you cooked, Dudley. You're a handy fella around the campfire."

"Thanks, Marshal."

"C'mon, Dudley. Help your old grandpa find that wagon bed."

"Okay." He went over and put his arm around the old man

and handed him a gnarled hickory cane. Remington couldn't help being touched by the sight of young Dudley supporting his gramps. "G'night, Marshal."

"Good night, Dudley. 'Night, Mr. Yates. Appreciate your help."

Remington walked over to where his horse was tethered, near the two grays. He reached down and picked up the coarse saddle blanket, unfolding it and shaking it out. Then he arranged his saddlebags, slicker, and other gear under it, finally topping it off with his black hat propped against the seat of his saddle. At that distance from the fire, it looked exactly like a sleeping man—which was how Remington wanted it to look.

Shadow eyed the hoax curiously. He had seen it a thousand times, yet each night it took him a few moments to realize it was not really Remington sleeping there. He gave a little snort and went back to his own sleep.

Using another blanket and a rolled-up shirt for a pillow, Remington bedded down a dozen yards away. With his black hair, dark clothes, and gray wool blanket, he faded into the shadows and became all but invisible. He had taken off his gunbelt, but the Colt was close at hand. The Henry rifle was within reach as well.

Remington squinted across the camp and in the firelight could see young Dudley helping his grandfather get settled in his bedroll in the back of the wagon.

These two were the kind Judge Barnstall had in mind when he preached about cleaning up this land for decent people, Remington reflected. They were the hard workers, the stiff spine of the country, the people who knew right from wrong and never let the two mix.

Ned Remington hated men like Snuff Tully. There was always evil in taking something that did not belong to you, especially if other people had earned it with their sweat, like the depositors at the bank Tully and his partners had robbed.

The outlaws in the Nations who knew of Judge Samuel Parkhurst Barnstall either shivered when they heard his name or cursed out loud. He recognized their evil and was pledged to stamp it out.

As much as he probably wanted to, Barnstall could not do

it alone. Remington knew where he fit in. He knew very well. He knew that Barnstall needed iron-hard men, men who were as fast as a diamondback and just as ready to strike.

Sometimes, on quiet nights like this one, when the stars seemed close enough for a man to reach out and grab, Remington wondered just what he would be doing if he had not pinned on the badge. He would not have gone wrong like Snuff Tully; he did not have the evil in him, never had. But he wondered where else he could earn his living with stony fists and a fast draw.

One thing was sure. Ned Remington never pondered on his past. Never gave much thought to the future, either, except to be careful enough to have one.

"Marshal?"

Dudley Yates did not see the blanket move. If he had, he would have suspected that there was a pistol under it, pointed at him. When Remington saw who it was, he lowered the barrel.

"What are you doing up yet, Dudley? Your grandpa's got a big day planned for you tomorrow. You've got a lot of miles to make."

"I know. I just . . . well, I had a feeling you might be gone when we wake up, so I just wanted to tell you thanks."

"Thanks for what, boy?"

"Thanks for talking to my grandpa, for asking for his help against this Tully. I sort of take care of Gramps now, have for the past few years. People don't treat him so good now that he's blind. Almost like he ain't there, you know what I mean?"

"Yeah."

"Gramps was an important man once. You made him feel important again tonight. He told me that just before he went to sleep. He said he felt good."

"I'll tell you something, Dudley. I don't know how a man could feel any better than to have a fine grandson like you."

"Thank you, sir."

"You know about the trip to Denver, don't you?"

"Yeah. I overheard Gramps telling Pa about it. I . . . I'm, scared, Marshal."

Remington propped himself up on one elbow and pointed his finger at the lad. "I didn't want to say anything to your grandpap, Dudley, but I think he's got it figured all wrong."

"What do you mean?"

"I'm no doctor, but I've got a strong feeling you don't have anything serious wrong with your eyes at all."

"But—"

"Doesn't it seem to get worse in the spring and summer? Sometimes fall?"

"Yeah."

"When winter comes, you just about think you're cured, until spring comes again."

"How'd you know?"

"I've seen it before," said Remington. "Don't know the name for it, but I knew a woman in Missouri who had the same thing. And let me tell you, boy, she never went blind. She lived to be eighty-four, and she was reading the Bible up to the day she died."

"Really?"

Even in the dim light, Remington could see the boy stand up taller. "Yep. I'll bet you're going to get good news up in Denver. You get to bed now. And take good care of your grandpa. We need men like him."

Chapter Five

Remington was making good time toward Salt Wells. As usual, he had gotten up an hour before dawn, cleaned up his bedroll, packed his gear, and hit the trail.

Remington had been impressed by Dudley Yates's courage. It was something he had learned from his grandfather, by watching the quiet strength in the man. Over the years, Remington had become something of an expert on courage. He knew that the bravery, the fortitude, of the old man was the real thing, not the recklessness born in a cavalry charge or the bravado of a shoot-out. Courage like that Herman Yates possessed was a quality to be envied.

Midmorning, Remington stopped by another narrow stream and breakfasted on crackers and pemmican. He stretched his legs, tightened and loosened the muscles in his thighs, in his back.

Late afternoon found him at the edge of Salt Wells. There was an impermanence to the town that he sensed right away. He had seen places like this before, dozens of them. Half were already gone, their main streets choked with tumbleweeds and brambles.

The buildings were what caught his attention. They were frame and clapboard, some so rickety that they threatened to cave in at the slightest wind. Years ago they had been painted; now they looked more like they were just made out of colored wood. Here was a dull green one, there a faded red; a few were covered with whitewash so old that it was the shade of broken-off deer antlers found in the woods. There was no railroad here, so they were not flatcar buildings—portable structures hauled from place to place at the sign of a boom—but they might just as well have been.

The only motion was the periodic swishing of a horse's tail and a mangy dog sniffing at a pile of garbage.

Remington had seen towns like Salt Wells before. It was not far from the cattle trails. Cowboys might drift in here, flush with money from a long, dusty drive. Doubtless there would be people in Salt Wells to take care of them—bartenders, cardplayers, loose women.

The lawman's eyes flicked this way and that, picking up the slightest details of the place and filing them in his memory. It was a thing he always did upon entering a new city. He might have to find his way around in the dark, chasing someone—or being chased. The hitchrails, alleys, barrels, boardwalks, porches, all were noted and remembered. They would come back any time he chose to recall them.

One thing he was fairly sure of. There would be no law in Salt Wells, at least not the kind of law *he* represented. To be a sheriff in this town, a man would have to have more than a taint of corruption. He would need to ignore a lot of things. Remington could not be like that.

He saw a sign that read *Prairie Dog Saloon.* It was as good a place to start as any.

Swinging down from the saddle, he walked his horse to a rail and tied the reins. Out of habit, he loosened the Colt in its holster before he walked inside.

The inside of the Prairie Dog Saloon was as pathetic as the outside. The bar was no more than a rough oak plank on sawhorses. Tables and chairs, about a half dozen of them, looked as if they had been rescued from a dump. On the back wall was a big round mirror, but the rear of it had been scratched and scraped so that it had ugly black marks across it.

Every eye bored in on Remington as he walked over to the bar. He quickly counted eight people in the place, four at a table, three at the bar, and the bartender, a brown-haired fellow with blotchy skin on his forehead. The men looked tough, but only half of them wore guns. The others looked ready to take anything on with their bare fists.

Remington understood that there was one thing, and one thing only, that set him apart from them. There was one thing that kept them from smiling or greeting him when he stepped into the room.

That was the U.S. marshal's badge pinned to his chest.

"I'm looking for a bank robber," he announced, loud enough for everyone to hear. The players had interrupted their card game the moment he came in. "His name's Snuff Tully."

Remington waited for the reaction. He could not predict what it might be, but he was ready for violence. His back was not exposed, and he could have his gun out in an instant.

"This Tully's an older man," he continued in an easy tone, in spite of their animosity. "He's in his sixties. Gray hair, something of a beard, about my size. Any of you seen him?"

He let his eyes trail from face to face. The weathered countenances told him nothing except that he should get out and quit bothering them.

Sometimes a man would talk but was afraid to do it in front of anybody else. If that were the case here, Remington decided, he would give any timid soul an opportunity. As it was, he was wasting his time asking them outright. Without another word, he backed toward the door.

Outside on the boardwalk, back leaning against the building, he waited ten minutes, wondering if someone would walk out behind him. No one came. Remington gave it up and continued up the street.

He had not taken ten steps when a fat man came out of a café. He was overflowing his pants, bulging out of his shirt. Food stains dotted his clothes. His star was rusty. It pulled down the pocket of his flannel shirt where it was fastened.

"Hey! Marshal! What are you doin' in Salt Wells?"

Remington was disgusted that this man could presume to call himself a peace officer. He appeared to be a hog disguised as a man.

"I'm trying to serve a bank-robbery warrant on a man named Snuff Tully. And I'm looking for an accomplice of his, Ramsey Clagg. I was told Tully is in your town."

The man's eyes widened a bit. He rubbed sausage-shaped

fingers across a stubbly beard, trying to feign hard thinking. Remington was not deceived.

"Ain't never heard of no Tully. 'Course, that don't mean nothin'. Folks ain't required to gimme their names when they come into town." He smiled on that, thinking it was quite clever.

Remington decided to conceal his revulsion. It was possible the man maintained *some* semblance of order, even in a place like this.

"Tully's in his sixties, gray hair, scruffy beard, about my size. That help any?"

The man contemplated the question. Remington could almost read what was going on in his mind: *It would not be wise to spill anything to this lawman first.* He would have to check with his bosses, the men who had him on the take, who pulled his puppet's strings.

"'Fraid I can't help you," he finally said.

"Didn't figure you would."

"I said I *can't.* There's a difference."

The gumption surprised Remington. Maybe this man had been a decent lawman once.

"You damn U.S. marshals. Who do you think you are, anyhow? I tried to get an appointment couple years ago. They wouldn't take me. Aw, the whole damn thing's political."

"And being a town sheriff—especially in a place like Salt Wells—isn't?" Remington had decided, on the spur of the moment, to bait him, to see how far he would go.

"I do my job."

"Which is to keep things under control just enough so they don't send *us* in to really clean things up."

"What's it to you? Ain't no decent folk in Salt Wells, anyway. Nobody's complainin' about how I do things."

"Fleecing the drovers is one thing," Remington said flatly. "Harboring a fugitive, especially a bank robber the likes of Snuff Tully, is another. I don't give a damn about your petty games, Sheriff. But when they interfere with my job, with enforcing the law, then there's going to be trouble."

"I said I don't know where he is."

Remington took a step closer. The fat man flinched but

tried to cover it. It was taking everything he had to stand up to this stranger.

"Here's a little friendly advice, from one lawman to another one," Remington said, cracking a humorless smile. "If you tip Tully, or tell somebody else and they warn him, so help me, I'll take you in in irons right beside him."

The sheriff's left cheek twitched. He took an uncertain step backward, then followed that with another, turning on his heel and retreating toward his office up the street.

Remington believed he had gotten his message across.

Another saloon took his eye, and he made for it. The sign above the door called it the Silver Spur, and it seemed to be the fanciest liquor parlor to be had in the dusty town.

The interior of the Silver Spur was a decided contrast to the Prairie Dog, just down the street. This place had a walnut bar, a few throw rugs on the floor, polished brass footrail and cuspidors, and a chandelier made of pieces of blue glass.

Despite the difference in atmosphere, the attitude was the same.

"Give me a beer," Remington told the barman, tossing a dime on the counter. Without speaking a word, the man filled a mug and set it before him. He was about to pick up the coin when Remington grabbed his hand. "I'm looking for a man named Snuff Tully, and another called Ramsey Clagg. They robbed a bank south of here. Clagg killed a deputy sheriff up in Kansas."

Reciting the charges had no effect on the man. At first he started to speak, then swallowed his comment and merely shrugged.

Remington was tempted to get rough with him. He knew Jake Virgil had given him straight information about the whereabouts of Tully. Being mannerly was not working.

Instinctively the bartender stepped back out of arm's reach and went down to another customer at the opposite end of the bar. Remington drank his beer.

He had known lawmen who would pull a gun out, shoot it into the ceiling, pistol-whip a man or two, then demand that someone talk. To his mind, that was buying trouble. And it was hard to enforce the law by breaking the law.

Still, he told himself, a trick like that sometimes worked.

The men in this place were better dressed and cleaner-looking than the toughs in the Prairie Dog. He guessed some of them might be the brains behind Salt Wells, maybe even the mayor or council leader, if such a place had one.

"I'm looking for a man," he said again, loud enough for the whole room to hear, though he felt he would get the same results shouting down a well. "His name is Snuff Tully. Him and two other fellas, Jake Virgil and Ramsey Clagg, robbed a bank south of here. Anybody who knows where Tully or Clagg is, I'd appreciate they'd tell me." Then, as an afterthought: "You want to do it on the QT, I'll be around town for a few more hours. I should be easy to find."

That said, he walked out. He did not bother waiting by the door, as he had at the other tavern. He might have misjudged them, but he did not see any friendlier faces in the Silver Spur.

There were other places yet to try. Hotels, stores, the livery stable. Asking questions was all part of the job, and so was getting no answers. Information—good, solid, useful information—was as rare and as precious as a nugget in a pan.

Remington returned to the place where he had tied his horse. He would take it over to the stable, have it fed and combed, and, at the same time, question the livery hand about Snuff Tully. He was determined to ask everyone in town if he had to. He had an undeniable hunch that Tully was still somewhere in Salt Wells.

"Mister?"

He turned to see a saloon girl, reddish hair, in a lacy, low-cut dress, standing on the boardwalk next to a building. Remington's face tightened. Her left eye was a hideous purple-blue, nearly swollen shut.

"Can I do something for you, miss?"

"I...I want to talk, about Tully. But not here. Not out in the open."

"Where, then? In your room?"

"No. Somebody might see you go in there. Back here. In the alley."

He tied the reins again and followed her down the narrow

passageway. He walked slowly, hugging the wall, checking the doorways. It might be a trap. He was a man who assumed every situation might be a trap. That was how he stayed alive.

When she turned to face him, Remington's hand was on the butt of his Colt. If she had a derringer, he could swat it out of her hand or, if need be, shoot her. But her hands were empty, folded cautiously at her waist.

"Now, what did you want to tell me about Tully, Miss . . ."

"Woodhouse. Clara Woodhouse."

At the back of the alley, where he had a chance to look at her better, Remington saw that she was a fairly handsome woman. Her face was somewhat plain, far from delicate, but he detected a definite kindness to it.

"My name's Ned Remington. I work out of Stone County, Missouri. What can you tell me about Tully, Miss Woodhouse?"

"I know where he is . . . or at least where he *might* be. I guess that's more than you've learned in Salt Wells so far. Folks aren't too friendly here."

"Where is he?"

"Last I heard, he was camped outside town, southwest, about two, three miles, in a rocky little canyon. On the Amarillo road. You shouldn't have any trouble finding the place. There are a lot of boulders and cliffs, rocks."

"Clagg with him?"

"No. All three of them were here at one time, but they split up. I haven't seen Virgil or Clagg since."

Remington had to ask the obvious question. "Why are you telling me this, Miss Woodhouse?"

She gave a wry grin. "You're not much on trust, are you? No, I don't expect you could be, in your business. It's not a trap, if that's what you're wondering. It should be obvious. See this shiner? Snuff Tully gave it to me."

"What happened?"

"I was . . . entertaining him up in my room. I wasn't especially happy about it, but, hell, it's what I do here. He wasn't like most of the cowboys who come in. Half of them are so damned shy I have to take their britches off for them. Anyhow, Tully started to get rough with me. Wanted me to . . .

well, let's just say I didn't want to do what he wanted me to. I don't do *that* for any man, for any amount of money. He was about half drunk. Started slapping me around. I tried to defend myself. He punched me in the eye. That knocked me out. Then he left."

"Doesn't that saloon have a bouncer to take care of you girls?"

She laughed, a short, sardonic chuckle. "It's not exactly like some knight in shining armor is defending our honor. Hell, I tried to scream, but Tully muffled me with a pillow. Let me tell you, Marshal, for an old bastard, he's pretty strong. Moves fast too."

"Thanks for the information. I wish I could pay you something, but I don't have the money for it."

"I don't want no money! You just bring that bastard in and see he gets put behind bars. That's all I want out of this."

"Thanks again." He gave a quick tug on the brim of his hat. "Oh, and about that eye? Make yourself a paste out of cold water and baking soda. Dab it around there, but try not to get it in your eye. It'll draw out the pain and make the swelling go down."

She looked at him in amazement, then said as he walked back toward the street, "You know, for a lawman, you're all right."

Remington gave a quick inspection of his horse. Shadow seemed in good shape, able to forgo the feeding and rest until after the trip out to Tully's camp. He took the reins in his hand and was just about to put his foot into the stirrup when three men came out of the Prairie Dog Saloon. Two wore guns, but they were dated models, pitted with rust, the holsters dry and cracked. A bowie knife was conspicuous on the third man's hip.

"You lookin' for Tully?"

"You know I am," Remington replied coolly. "You were in the saloon when I asked if anybody knew where he was." He backed away from his horse, casually flipping the leather thong off the hammer of his gun.

The man who spoke, a squat, thick-browed fellow, advanced a step. From the hunch of his shoulders, he looked like a man more used to settling his accounts with his fists than with a firearm.

Three against one was not good odds. Remington intended to even them before things got out of control.

"Some problem here, boys?"

Remington swiveled at the sound of the strange voice behind him. He was surprised to see the fat sheriff, a double-barreled shotgun in the crook of his left arm.

"This man's goin' after Tully," said the leader of the three.

"I reckon' he's got a right to," the sheriff replied. "He's a U.S. marshal, and Tully done robbed a bank south of here. Warrants are all in order. You boys throwin' in with Tully now?"

That question brought shifting gazes. It seemed to baffle them. Apparently they were not used to thinking quickly on their feet.

"'Cause if you are," the sheriff continued, "you're not only obstructin' justice, but you're aidin' and abettin' a fugitive too. That could mean a lot of years behind bars, fellas."

The imposing barrels of the scattergun and the deadly coolness of the marshal proved too overpowering for them. Their allegiance to Snuff Tully evaporated in light of their stronger urge for self-preservation. Slowly, cautiously, trying to save as much face as possible, they retreated into the saloon.

"Appreciate the help," Remington said, trying to keep the astonishment out of his voice.

"I been thinkin' about what you said," the big man answered. "Got back to my office and took a look in my shavin' mirror. Didn't like what I saw. I guess, if'n I was honest, I ain't liked it for a lot of years. You know, I been in Salt Wells too damn long, Marshal. I reckon if I get out now, maybe the stink of this place'll blow off of me."

"You're making the right move," Remington said. "Good luck to you, then."

The sheriff's mouth dropped open when the marshal extended his hand. The big man took it and shook it with a warm grip. "Thanks. Say, you want some help? I mean, if you found out where Tully is."

"No offense, but I work better alone. Always have. But I appreciate you backing my hand just now. You take care of yourself . . . lawman."

Remington swung up in the saddle and trotted the horse out of town. He could not suppress a grin. Just when he thought he was an infallible judge of character, somebody like the big sheriff came along to teach him otherwise.

Darkness had closed around Remington by the time he got to the little stony canyon that Clara Woodhouse had described. Massive boulders loomed here and there, solid, blacker shapes against the rest of the landscape. He dismounted and tied his horse to a bush.

He reached into his saddlebag and withdrew a small object. It was a brass nautical spyglass that extended to about a foot in length. He crept over to a group of stones by the canyon rim and put the telescope to his eye.

Only a thin yellow rind of a moon hung in the sky, providing poor illumination. The bigger rocks on the canyon floor stood out, but most of the rest of the scene was lost in blackness.

Remington scanned the terrain. The first sign of life he saw was Tully's horse, hobbled near a clump of brush. A bit more checking revealed a fire, or rather, a pit of hot coals. Old Herman Yates had been right. Tully *was* sneaky. He had built his fire during the daylight, let it die down so he could cook on the hot coals after dark. They were barely visible, whereas even a small flaming campfire would have been like a beacon. —

Snuff Tully was nowhere around. Remington looked for a bedroll, but there was none. Maybe the man was off somewhere, relieving himself. Remington waited another fifteen minutes. Tully did not return.

By this time, Remington had come up with a plan.

Snuff Tully heard the sound of approaching hoofbeats on the hard gravel floor of the canyon. Every night he did the same thing, and tonight it was going to pay off.

He had had to ride the whole canyon before he found the

campsite he wanted. This one was perfect. He pulled the blanket up around him.

The spot where he was hiding was not actually a cave but more of a large crevice. From it he could see his horse, his camp, the bed of coals, and much of the canyon stretched in front of him. The inside of the crevice was as dark as soot.

He was completely hidden. It was an ideal spot to ambush somebody.

Just like he was going to shoot this approaching rider. Maybe the man would have something of value in his pockets or in his saddlebags. At the very least, he could sell the dead man's horse and saddle and guns.

Tully peered out into the night. He could make out a shape, the general silhouette of a black horse.

There was no rider!

Tully had to control himself to keep from chuckling. This man was a smart one. He sent his horse in ahead of himself. Tully watched the big black. It paused a moment in his camp, sniffing at the ground, then ambled over to where his own horse was tied.

Patience would win this one for him. Tully had the sand to wait this one out. Even if the man came in and started poking around, he would hold off until he had a clear, killing shot. It would be like blasting chickens inside a henhouse.

A noise, barely audible but distinct nonetheless, reached Snuff Tully's ears. Tully smiled. He cocked the hammer of his big Sharps rifle. The man was coming. The stupid bastard would never know what took the top of his skull off.

Then there was another sound, not the scraping of a boot-heel or the rustle of clothing, but of a friction match being lit.

Tully looked for the flame, planning to sight in on it. He put the rifle butt to his shoulder. But he saw no orange glow out in that darkness.

A crackling, sputtering noise caught his ears. He had heard it sometime in the past, but he could not identify it without seeing what made it.

Good Lord!

It came down into the crevice where he was hiding, a hissing, jumping, burning dynamite fuse. It hit the side wall, bounced off, skittered down the other.

He grabbed for it, but it had slid down into a fissure he could not fit his hand into. Tully had no idea how long that fuse was. If it was a short one, his life would be over in seconds.

Tully jumped through the mouth of the crevice.

The single shot sounded as soon as he was out. He felt his right hand go numb. The Sharps clattered to the ground.

"Drop your sidearms and knives. All of them!" barked a voice from the darkness.

He tried to home in on it, but it was futile. The man had been able to shoot him in the hand in such dim light. Tully realized he was covered. Trying anything now would mean the end of him. He tossed his other weapons in front of him and raised his hands.

"Make one move, Tully, and you're a dead man."

The black specter glided out of the shadows, Colt pointed at his prisoner. Tully took in the dark hair, mustache, black clothing and hat. He caught the glint of the silver badge.

"Chief Territorial Marshal Remington out of Stone County, Missouri. I'm arresting you for the bank robbery you and Virgil and Clagg pulled in south Texas."

"Hey," Tully said, glancing anxiously back at the crevice. "What happened to that dynamite? When's it gonna go off?"

"Dynamite?" Remington gave a short laugh. "Never was no dynamite, Tully. That stuff's expensive. I just keep a handful of fuses in my saddlebags, for situations like this one."

The old man swore under his breath. If only he had waited it out.

"Put these manacles on, Tully," said the marshal, tossing a set of irons at the outlaw's feet. "We're leaving."

"In the middle of the night? Where?"

"Amarillo. They've got a jail there ought to hold you. Till I come back for you."

"Back from where?" he asked as he clamped the heavy irons on his wrists.

"From getting Ramsey Clagg. I already got Jake Virgil. And I just got you."

"Mister, you ain't bit off the biggest chaw yet."

"Where is he?"

"Why should I tell you?"

"'Cause Virgil told me where you were. I figured you'd want to do Clagg the same favor."

Tully snorted. "Hell, why should I try to hold out? Likely you'd just dump a panful of them hot coals down my pants if I didn't tell. But your knowin' ain't gonna do you a damn bit of good."

Remington watched with satisfaction as the steel-grated door was closed on Tully in the Amarillo jail. He walked down the corridor with the jailer back to the main office.

"That Tully's been raising hell for years," the older man said. "You were lucky to come out of that alive, Marshal."

"He's the one who was lucky," Remington corrected. "Our judge doesn't cotton to us bringing in corpses."

"Where'd Tully say Clagg is hiding out?"

"Place in the mountains, couple days west of here. He called it Hell's Door."

The jailer whistled. "Do you know what that is?"

"Tully told me."

"And you're still going? By yourself?"

Remington replied with only a silent nod as he stepped through the front door back into the sunlight. He wanted to shave, get a bath, and catch up on his sleep before he set out. After all, there was no hurry now.

Ramsey Clagg had the mistaken notion that he was safe.

Chapter Six

For Chief Territorial Marshal Ned Remington, eating breakfast in a sit-down café, off of real china, was an unheard-of luxury.

Deprivation, hardship, discipline were a way of life for him, yet he would just as quickly turn around and indulge himself. Ned Remington made a terrific effort to keep from becoming predictable, for he knew such a trait could mean the end of a working lawman.

His only routine was one of caution. Men who expected him to be in a certain place at a regular time were invariably disappointed. Men who expected him to slip the hammer thong off his Colt getting ready for a draw were astonished when he mysteriously produced a derringer and got the drop on them.

He mopped up the remainder of his egg yolk with a piece of biscuit. By the time he finished, it looked as if he had been served only a clean, empty plate.

"I'll have to say one thing for you, Marshal," voiced the waitress, a freckle-faced, rusty-haired girl about twenty. "You sure do justice to a breakfast."

"That's 'cause it's such a welcome change from my own cooking. You got some more coffee?"

"Sure. Just a minute." She left, then returned with a big blue enameled pot. She filled his cup to the top.

"Thanks."

"I don't think I've ever seen you in Amarillo before, Marshal. Not that you mightn't have been here, of course. It's a pretty big town."

"Yeah, it is," Remington agreed, measuring the girl. She had outgrown her gangliness and was starting to become pretty. In another year or two she would be a real head turner.

"You hunting somebody? I mean, we get U.S. marshals in town once in a while, but usually they're after somebody."

"I'm tracking a killer named Ramsey Clagg. I'm going out after him this morning." Remington was beginning to realize that her interest in him was more than casual.

"Can't say I've ever heard of that one," the girl said as she cleared the dishes onto a tray. "Gossip gets around, you know, about who's done what to who. But I don't recall that name."

"He killed a deputy sheriff up in Kansas, robbed a bank in south Texas."

"Oh. Well, good luck to you, Marshal. You be careful, hear?"

Watching the sway of her hips as she walked away, Remington wished he could stay in Amarillo longer. But it seemed that was how it always turned out. He paid his tab and left her a quarter tip—twice as much as usual. Hell, he smiled to himself, it was worth that much just to see those big green eyes and that bucktoothed grin of hers.

After he retrieved Shadow from the livery stable, he wasted little more time in Amarillo. The mount was in excellent shape: frisky, well fed, eager to put a lot of ground under his hooves. For that alone, the delay had been worth it. Remington was a man who took faultless care of his horse. If there was an ounce of sentimentality in the lawman at all, it was toward the black gelding. But there was a practical side to it as well. More than once his life had been saved because his horse was strong and rested and the other man's was not. Those were lessons Remington never forgot.

He fished Pete Trask's map out of his shirt pocket. No indication was on it as to the location of Hell's Door, but the jailer in Amarillo had pointed out the general direction. Borders were uncertain in this part of the country. They made no difference to him anyway, as long as he was riding for Judge Samuel Parkhurst Barnstall. He had the wanted posters, and his badge, and the warrants signed by the stocky jurist. That was all the authority he needed.

No lawman worth his salt would argue with that.

The capture of Snuff Tully had turned out all right. It could just as easily have gone the other way, although Remington had taken every precaution he could think of. Even a smart man like Tully made a mistake once in a while. As far as Ned Remington was concerned, Tully had made his *last* mistake.

As he rode along, it crossed the marshal's mind that Tully, even now sitting in that cramped Amarillo jail cell, might be having the last laugh. The chase for Clagg into the mountains might be a wild-goose run. The place called Hell's Door was a couple days' ride at least. Maybe Tully had illusions that Clagg, or somebody, would bust him out of that Amarillo cage. If that was what he thought, he was not as smart as Remington had first assumed.

Snuff Tully was a story already told. The one yet for the telling was the capture of Ramsey Clagg. A hundred times, Remington had rolled the description and poster sketch through his mind, just as he had with Tully and Virgil. Clagg was a real man for him. He had formed a picture of the buffalo hunter, tall, well over six feet, a giant in size, going over three hundred pounds. His hair was long and scraggly, as was his beard. Both were the color of dried carrot peelings. His right eye was brown, his left eye gray. Scars crossed his face like dried-up riverbeds. The pinkie finger on his left hand was missing the first joint.

Clagg usually wore loose, baggy clothes, from the accounts of witnesses. His hat had a wide brim and a round crown. Sometimes he stuck a brace of crow's feathers in the side of the band.

Befitting his size, he carried a pair of massive Walker Colts, still in percussion style. He carried the Sharps rifle he had shot buffalo with, but he was also known to use a Spencer repeater.

The murder of Pete Trask had told Remington the most important thing he needed to know about Ramsey Clagg. The man was as sadistic as he was dangerous and had a smoldering hatred for peace officers.

It would take every bit of Ned Remington's wits to bring him in alive.

With Shadow setting a fast pace, the miles seemed to go by quickly. For the first several hours, the country was plains—flat, with an occasional gully or wash.

Remington knew he was somewhere between the Canadian and Pecos rivers, heading generally northwest. He could finger it on his map, but he had never been in this area before. The spindly creosote bushes and spike-leaved ocotillo were giving way to twisted pinyon pines as he rode into a higher elevation. He was momentarily startled when a small herd of pronghorn antelope bounded a few dozen yards ahead of him.

It was becoming more rugged. The flatland was gone; ahead lay the mountains. He swung down southwest again, following the pencil scratchings he had made on the map. Soon he would not be able to shift and turn at will; he would need to know where the passes were.

Remington camped before dark. Again he pulled the old scheme of laying out the phony bedroll, wondering even as he did it whether it was becoming too much of a habit. If he were realistic, he would have admitted that there was probably no one within fifty miles. In an odd way, though, it made him sleep better.

The next day's riding brought him higher into the mountains, and the day after that took him higher still. The ruggedness was interrupted by a rare piece of flat ground. Remington sat his horse at the top of a ridge, a stand of firs behind him to break up his silhouette.

The air was as fresh and clean as a drink of ice water. Remington sucked in deeply, detecting a faint aroma of pine needles. A pair of red-tailed hawks wheeled around the sky overhead, their wings a stark contrast against the big, fluffy clouds.

Remington looked out across the flat and was surprised to see a house there. No smoke was coming from the chimney, so he had momentarily overlooked it.

It was more refined than a log cabin, though it was not painted. Shakes covered the roof, a few missing here and there, some covered with a dark green moss. There was glass in the windows and white curtains. The barn, not far away, *was* a log structure, as were three or four smaller buildings.

The place had a strange loneliness to it, out in these mountains all by itself. It was almost as if it had fallen from the sky.

Less than a dozen cattle grazed in a stony pasture. Crops in a rock-infested field were waging a gallant struggle to stay alive.

Despite the lushness of the trees and nearby grass, the spread had an air of desolation about it. Remington felt the skin at the nape of his neck pucker as a cool breeze filtered through the pines.

He walked his horse carefully down the hill, avoiding the rocks and small boulders that protruded through the soil.

He looked for signs of life but saw none. As he got closer to the house he wondered about the wisdom of his decision to move down. He would have been wiser to bypass the outfit altogether.

"Get offa that horse and you're a dead man."

The voice was like a slap in the face. Remington had seen no one on his way in. His quick scan of the house and the barn and the outbuildings revealed no one.

Closer inspection of a grazing cow disclosed a rifle barrel lying across its back and a pair of man's legs behind the animal. How had he missed that before?

The head sticking up was bald and shiny. One thing was certain: It was not the red-topped Ramsey Clagg.

"Name's Remington," he shouted. "I'm a U.S. marshal out of Stone County, Missouri."

"Missouri? What the hell you doin' way out here?"

"I'm looking for a killer," Remington returned. "And unless your name is Ramsey Clagg, you can put that gun down."

There was silence for several seconds. The gun did not move. Then, very slowly, the muzzle went up in the air and the man held it up as he came around the cow and walked through the corral. The man looked to be in his mid-forties, with a tired face and a slow, determined walk. He wore the rough blue shirt of a farmer and pants with leather braces. In his right hand was the gun, in the other a galvanized bucket of milk.

"I was out milkin' when you rode up," the farmer explained. "I hid amongst the cows, kept a bead on you from the time you started down that hill. Wasn't sure you was really a lawman till I saw the sun reflectin' off that badge just now."

Remington climbed out of the saddle as the man walked over.

"You had a right to challenge me."

"My name's Elson O'Keefe," the farmer said, holding out a big, rawboned hand. Remington shook it.

"Ned Remington."

"I never heard of a marshal comin' all the way from Missoura to this place after a man, even if he is a killer."

"You don't know our judge," Remington said.

"He must be one ornery bastard."

"That he is, that he is."

"Well, I'm forgettin' my manners, Marshal. Guess I been forgettin' a lot of things lately. Lead your horse over to the trough there, and come on in the house. I'll scare us up somethin' to eat."

"I appreciate the hospitality, Mr. O'Keefe. It's been a long ride."

"Never mind that 'mister' stuff, Marshal. Elson suits me fine. Ain't nobody ever called me mister in my life."

Despite the man's jolly demeanor, there was an unmistakable sadness in his eyes. He had one of those faces whose overly large features combined into an image of gentleness. Lines and wrinkles appeared at the corners of his eyes when he smiled.

Remington had a feeling the farmer was smiling even though he did not feel like it.

Once inside the house, Remington immediately deduced that Elson O'keefe had not done the decorating. From the lace on the curtains to the checkered tablecloth to the ceramic knickknacks on a shelf, it was evident that a woman had put her hand in it.

"Hope your wife doesn't mind me just barging in unannounced like this," Remington said.

"She's gone," O'Keefe replied; then he sank heavily onto a kitchen chair, as if all the weight of the world were pressing down on him.

"She left you?"

"She was murdered."

"By who?"

"A man came through here a couple weeks ago. I don't know his name. Probably wouldn't matter if I did. It was just before suppertime, late afternoon. He came riding in. Hell, I didn't suspect nothin'. We never had any trouble with strangers before. Usually we gave them a meal and they slept in the barn overnight.

"This fella was different. He got down off his horse, I held out my hand to shake his, and he punched me in the face. It knocked me down right away. When I started to get up, he kicked me, then started beatin' on me with his fists. All the time I could hear Sarah screamin'. Wasn't nothin' she could do. Hell, wasn't nothin' *I* could do. He caught me by surprise, then kept at me till I was near unconscious."

"He didn't say anything? Didn't give you any warning or reason at all?"

"I found out the reason, but by then it was too late. After he finished with me—or thought he had—he started on my Sarah."

"He beat your wife?"

"No. He raped her. Right in front of my eyes."

Sometimes even Remington heard something that he found difficult to fathom. "You saw it?"

"I guess he thought he'd killed me. He might as well have. I was on the ground, a dozen yards away, hangin' there between conscious and unconscious. I'd watch, then I'd black out, then I'd come to again. I couldn't move. I couldn't even yell. I tried to, but, dammit, nothin' came out. I tried to crawl, but I couldn't seem to get any strength in my arms."

"Then what happened?"

"After he was done with Sarah, he went in the house," the farmer continued. "He beat her up some too, 'cause she fought him. He turned everything upside down and stole what little money we had. Took some fruit Sarah had canned. Then the son of a bitch rode off, just like he came, leaving us both there."

"Don't you have any neighbors?"

O'Keefe shook his head. "Not for miles. We both laid

there, all that day and all that night. The next morning, I put
the little strength I had together and crawled my way over to
Sarah. He . . . he musta really worked her over, 'cause she was
dead." Then his eyes glazed over. "God, Marshal, she was the
only woman I ever loved."

Remington could not believe what he had heard. It was like
a nightmare coming true. He sat down opposite Elson
O'Keefe.

"Did you tell the law about this?"

"Hell, there ain't no law in these parts. That's why that
bastard did what he did, knowin' full well he could get away
with it scot-free."

"What did he look like?" Remington asked.

O'Keefe ran a hand across his face and his bald head. A
great weariness had transformed him from a forty-year-old
into an old man. "He was a big fella. A monster. Biggest man
I ever seen. Had red hair and a red beard."

The lawman tried to keep his face impassive. He did not
want O'Keefe to know the redheaded man was the same one
he was tracking—Ramsey Clagg.

"Which direction did he ride off?" Remington inquired.

"Don't matter. There's only one way out of this valley, and
that's the way you come in. After a man gets on the other side
of the ridge, he can go whatever way he pleases. So, no, I
can't tell you which way he headed. Why? Are you goin' after
him?" There was a tinge of disbelief in the farmer's voice. He
was a man who had been broken one too many times.

"I've got a job to do," Remington answered, "a job I came
all the way from Missouri for. After I get it done, then we'll
see."

"Well," O'Keefe said, "at least you're honest enough not to
promise what you can't deliver."

"So you didn't go to the law? You haven't told anybody
else about this?"

"Took me two, almost three weeks just to recover from that
beatin' he gave me. I was lucky I could take care of my
animals, Marshal. No. I haven't been off this spread since it
happened."

"If you scout up some supper for us, I'd be glad to do your chores," Remington said.

"By God, I'm not gonna turn down an offer like that. Make sure there's water in the animals' troughs, and get the chickens in and close the henhouse door. We'll need a bucket or two of water from the pump, and how about choppin' some wood for breakfast cookin' tomorrow morning?"

"It's done." Remington started to go out toward the barn.

"Hey, Marshal. You can leave that hogleg here, if you want to."

"Nope. I don't go anywhere without it. Just like you keep that old Spencer with you now."

"Yeah. Too bad I had to learn the hard way."

The supper Elson O'Keefe prepared them was solid and edible—a beef stew—but it had little taste. All through the meal, the farmer apologized for it.

"Sorry the food's not better, Marshal. Sarah . . . she did all the cookin'. I never really learned. Guess it shows."

"It's hot and there's plenty of it. What more could a man want?" Remington asked.

"If you'd ever tasted my Sarah's chicken and dumplings, then you'd know what real cookin' is like. Don't imagine you get many home-cooked meals, being a lawman out on the trail. You married?"

"No."

"How long you been a marshal?"

"Seems like all my life, Elson."

"Yeah. That's the way it's been with me and farmin' too. I wasn't always a farmer, though. Used to work in a hardware store over in Santa Fe. That's where I met Sarah. It was always her dream to live on a farm. We sure picked us a godforsaken place."

"I'll bet you were real happy here once."

Elson O'Keefe thought about it. "We were. Sure. Happiest I've ever been in my life."

"Looks like sort of a hard scrabble, though. Was that corn I saw growing in that field over north?"

"Yeah, and wheat next to that. We'll get the rain for it up here. Sometimes the growing season can be short. But everybody has good years and bad years. Hell, I bet even lawmen have hard times when people behave themselves."

"I never really thought about it that way," Remington returned. "I guess if everybody *did* obey the law, I'd be out of a job."

"Marshal?"

"Yeah?"

"You'll . . . sorta overlook my whinin' and complainin', huh? I mean, I ain't normally a complainer, but, Jesus, my life just dried up and turned to dust since Sarah died."

"I understand, Elson. Maybe it's best, you talking about it to me. You've had it bottled up inside you too long."

"I was hopin' this afternoon when you rode down that hill, I was hopin' that you was that big redheaded bastard come back. I was gonna blow him out of the saddle—but just wound him. Then I was gonna make him pay for what he done to my Sarah. For what he done to me."

"You wouldn't want to do that," Remington said, taking two small cigars from his inside vest pocket and handing one to the farmer. He lit them both. "That'd make you as bad as him."

"But you . . ."

"I take my prisoners in alive, even though most of them need killing and need it real bad. I think our judge, old Sam Barnstall, understands that he can't send out a pack of wolves to wreak vengeance on these men, even if they deserve it. There has to be law, and the worse the crime, the worse the law is needed. You get what I'm saying?"

"I don't know. That's all right for Barnstall to say. All right for you to say, even. But when it hits home, when somethin' like this happens to you, then we'll see how you feel about the law."

"Maybe you're right," Remington admitted. "All I know is that it seems more right when a jury finds a man guilty of a crime and a court sends him to the gallows, rather than shooting him down like a mad dog. If I didn't believe in it, Elson, I couldn't wear this star."

"Marshal, it's been a long day. I'm about ready to turn in. I'm just going to put these dishes in a pan on the sideboard here, then take care of them and the breakfast dishes tomorrow."

"I'll sleep in the barn," Remington volunteered. "I saw a bunk out there that looked pretty inviting. I just want to finish this cheroot before I sack in."

"G'night, then."

"See you in the morning, Elson."

Remington sat on a wooden bench outside the barn, looking up at the stars, thinking for a long time. He did not want Elson O'Keefe going with him after Clagg. The farmer wanted revenge, pure and simple, and that was the quickest way to get killed. Remington was a professional at this. He did not need a slow hand or bad shot along, making it that much tougher for him.

The truth of the farmer's words haunted Remington. He wondered if Judge Barnstall had ever experienced a tragedy like this himself. Then again, maybe he had. Maybe his iron-clad adherence to the letter of the law was his way of keeping himself from slipping over that dangerous line.

In the morning, Remington did the chores while O'Keefe prepared the meal. Breakfast proved to be considerably tastier than supper—sausage, scrambled eggs, and hash brown potatoes.

After the meal, Remington went outside to tend to his horse while O'Keefe attacked the mound of dishes. He made short work of them, stacking them in a white pine cupboard. Then he came out of the house, standing on the front porch, wiping his hands on a towel.

"I'd like to ask you another favor," Remington said, leading the gelding over.

"What do you need?"

"I'm heading into some rough country, an outlaw camp. It wouldn't be smart for me to wear my badge into there, or even to keep it in my saddlebags. I'd like you to hold on to it for me for safekeeping. I'll pick it up on my way back." He unpinned the badge and put it in O'Keefe's hand.

"I'd be proud to. That's . . . that's a mighty dangerous thing you're doin', Marshal. You must think pretty high of this Barnstall."

"Yeah. But I'm not doing it for him. I'm doing it for the family of the deputy that Clagg killed. I'm doing it for the ranchers and farmers who had money in that bank he robbed. I guess, in a way, I'm doing it for myself, too. If I can scrape some of the scum off this earth and put it where it belongs, then it makes me feel a lot better."

The two men walked from the shade of the porch to the center of the farmyard. Before Remington mounted, he noticed O'Keefe looking toward the top of the hill, off to the south, near a stand of pines. The marshal followed the farmer's gaze.

Atop the hill was a whitewashed board cross.

As both men watched, a mountain chickadee flapped down and landed on one of the crossarms of the grave marker.

"Damn birds," O'Keefe said quietly. "Sarah used to leave stale bread and suet out for them in the winter. Looks like they can't forget her either." Then his eyes misted over. "Damn birds," he whispered.

"I'll find the man that did it," Remington swore. "I'll bring him to justice, Elson." They shook hands. "Thanks for all your hospitality. Remember, I'll be back for that badge."

"You be careful, Marshal."

Remington was another hour into the hills before he realized that to come back and pick up his badge, he would have to bring Ramsey Clagg with him to the O'Keefe farm. That might present problems, but it also might convince O'Keefe that he had not been lying and that Clagg would, indeed, face Sam Barnstall's unwavering justice.

As for the warrants and the wanted posters, Remington intended to hide them somewhere along the trail. He could not have turned them over to O'Keefe. If the farmer looked through them, he would have known immediately that the man who raped his wife and the man Remington was after were one and the same.

Remington felt naked without his badge. It was as much a part of him as his hat or his gunbelt—even more so. He did not relish playing the part of an outlaw, but he knew it was necessary if he wanted to bring Clagg out and stay alive.

Two murders. Two brutal, senseless, sadistic murders.

It would take some willpower not to draw on Clagg, or to put him under before they got back to the Galena courtroom. The man needed killing.

Remington hoped he would be able to wait until the hangman could do it.

Chapter Seven

Remington was certain he was in the general area of the legendary outlaw camp known as Hell's Door, but despite all of his tracking skill, he was unable to find the trail into it.

He had backtracked most of the afternoon, following hoof-prints and even wagon tracks from where they jumbled together to a point where they split up or abruptly ended.

In a few hours it would be dark. He could camp on a peak, on the odd chance that he would spot a rider coming out, but he was not even sure he was within miles of the place. A dozen times he had consulted Trask's well-worn map. Hell's Door was not on it.

Remington had heard of it several times before in his years as a lawman, but he had always dismissed the stories as myth. The thought that Snuff Tully might have sent him on a wild-goose chase suddenly came back to him.

O'Keefe's story about Clagg raiding his farm fit in, though. Tully, Virgil, and Clagg had split up after the robbery; then Clagg left Salt Wells after that. He must have swung by the O'Keefe farm on his way to Hell's Door.

The marshal was about to head for higher ground when he heard voices, very faint, in the distance. He guided his horse into a clump of trees and dismounted. Holding the reins, he patted the gelding's snout with his other hand, a signal to the horse that he was to keep quiet.

Remington pulled his little spyglass out of his saddlebag. The sounds continued through the valley. The men who were talking obviously felt that they were far enough in the middle of nowhere that they could abandon some caution.

The size of the band also gave them some confidence. Remington counted thirteen of them. Judging from their sombreros and cartridge belts, he figured them for Comancheros.

He was in luck. They were not coming out of the valley but going into it. They were headed for Hell's Door.

After the men were out of sight and their voices barely audible, Remington mounted up again and took up their trail. He could not lose them.

Another two hours they rode. The path was a twisting, turning one, coming back on itself like a snake shedding skin. Finally Remington learned the secret. They entered a shallow creek and rode in the center of it for nearly two miles. He ventured closer to them, close enough so he could see them.

From the cover of a bankside willow, he watched them walk their horses out of the creek onto a rocky ledge. Even horseshoes would not leave a mark on it. The ledge ran about five hundred feet on a diagonal from the stream; then it connected with a gravel flat.

The Comancheros were far up the trail by the time Remington led Shadow across the stone ledge. He was doubly cautious in case the outlaws had left a man behind.

After he got across the gravel, he had no trouble picking up the group's trail again. It doubled back once more, through a sandy clearing, then headed straight into a canyon.

Darkness had fallen. Remington continued to follow, more on a hunch than from what he could see. He saw occasional bent blades of grass, the lightest outline of a horseshoe, but the trail was remarkably thin.

The country had become more severe, laced with cliffs and pillars, gravelly hills, harsher plants and cactus. It seemed a fitting place for the most dangerous men in the country to hide.

More voices and noise told Remington he was close. He decided to stop for about an hour. It would not be wise to enter the camp right on the Comancheros' heels.

Leaving the place in the daylight would be considerably easier, but getting out at night could be tricky. He was still not certain of his directions, even though he had a rough idea from the stars. Going out, he would not have to worry about finding the trail. Any way out was fine, as long as it did not lead him into a box canyon.

Hell's Door proved to be a surprise. He had not expected buildings, yet there they were. He had expected to find maybe a few dozen men. Just the ones he saw out and about came to well over a hundred, and there were women and a few children as well.

No one paid any attention to him as he rode in. Without the badge, he did not look that much different from the rest of them. He had seen no guards at the perimeter, at least none who had accosted him.

The buildings were log cabins and rough-hewn board, nothing elaborate. A few had glass windows; most had oilcloth or canvas. There were many tents. As he rode up the dirt street Remington saw one of the women close up and confirmed his suspicions. She was rough-looking, spent, probably chased out of most decent towns, too old to work as a saloon girl. Maybe she had been one of the camp followers of Fighting Joe Hooker's army six or seven years ago.

A couple of the men cast wary eyes at Remington. He had to tell himself several times that nobody here had any way of knowing who he was, what he was.

He tried to make some sense of the place, but it was hopeless in the dark. A torch burned here and there and an occasional lantern hung from a post. His nose led him to one of the log cabins. He realized one of the women must be operating it as an eating place.

Remington dismounted, tied up his horse, then took his Henry rifle and his saddlebags with him as a precaution. He was, after all, in a town of thieves.

"What'll it be? We got beef stew and we got chicken stew tonight," a fat woman with a wart on her nose spoke as soon as he stepped inside the door. "Bread comes with both."

Beef stew was probably made from old horses. The worst thing in the chicken stew could be jackrabbits or prairie dogs.

"Make it chicken stew," Remington said.

"Fifty cents—in advance."

"That's kind of steep, isn't it?"

She let out a hoarse laugh, and he saw that half her teeth

were missing. "Fella, this must be your first time in Hell's Door."

"So?"

"So this is the only eat place here. You either buy from me or cook your own stuff. Now, you paying the fifty cents or ain't you?"

He dug in a pocket and handed her a pair of quarters. She ladled into a big pot on the cookstove and dished him up a bowlful of a yellowish brown goo. He recognized a carrot tip and several potato chunks. Maybe it was just as well that the meat was scarce. She gave him a big hunk of break, a knife and fork.

"Coffee to wash it down with?"

"Yeah."

"A dime."

He paid. She handed him a large tin cup. At least the coffee smelled palatable.

"And I don't want you stealing none of them utensils when you're done," she snapped. "Bring them back to me. Don't leave them laying on the table."

He took a seat on a bench at one of the tables. The room was small enough that most of the diners were within arms' reach of one another.

"Howdy, boys," he said flatly as he sat down.

They nodded mutely. One mumbled something that was either a greeting or a belch. Remington did not pursue it. He made no move to introduce himself and knew that none of them would either. The marshal had to remind himself that these men were on the run, suspicious of everyone and everything.

"Ain't never seed you in Hell's Door before," one of them ventured.

Remington glanced up at the man. "First time for me here."

"Where'd *you* hear about it?" another man asked.

"Pal of mine. Jake Virgil. Maybe you heard of him."

"Yeah. I know Jake," said a man with dirty blond hair. "How's he doin'? I ain't seen him since we worked deckhand on a riverboat during the war."

"Jake was never no sailor that I knew of," Remington said quietly. "He's a buffalo hunter, and a damn good one too."

The blond man grinned with tobacco-stained teeth.

"Guess you're right, mister. Virgil *is* a buffalo hunter. I musta been thinkin' of somebody else."

The ruse was so transparent that it was stupid. Remington had been expecting something like this. He continued eating his meal, as if he had not caught on.

"How's come you're at Hell's Door?" a thick-browed man asked. The fellow was using his sleeve as a napkin. Brown gravy spotted his cuff.

Remington gave him an ice-cold glare. "You ought to know better than to ask a question like that."

"Yeah, it *was* pretty dumb," the blond man chimed in.

If the people at Hell's Door exchanged names, they were probably phony ones. Although they had banded here together to escape from the law, no man could be sure that the other was not a Judas. Remington picked up the attitude right away. No one gave his real name and no one answered questions about his crimes.

"You ever hunted buffalo?" Remington asked the blond man. It was a safe subject to pursue.

"I done some of everything. Skinned out hides. Cut out buffalo tongues and vitals for pickling. Even picked bones a season or two. Didn't like it, though. You get a stink on you takes a year to wash off."

Remington thought the man had still not succeeded. He reeked of stale sweat and strong tobacco. He must have been a stranger to a bathtub or a stream.

"I'm looking for a buffalo hunter," Remington stated. "He's a big fella, a head taller than you. Real heavy. He's got red hair and a red beard. Seen him hereabouts?"

"Sure," Blondie answered. "That there's Ramsey Clagg you described. Everybody in camp knows him."

"He use his real name?" Remington tried to act surprised.

"Hell, yes. Clagg ain't afraid of nobody. If you know him, you know why."

"I don't know him," Remington responded. He swiped up the last bit of yellow gravy from his bowl with a morsel of bread and popped it into his mouth. "I've heard of him. I might have some business to do with him."

"Clagg plays cards a lot," said the thick-browed eater. "Likely a game goin' right now. That's where you'll find him, prob'ly."

"Good. You boys take care of yourself, hear? And make sure you give your stuff back to that old bat. I'll bet she's got a scattergun filled with rock salt she uses on stealers."

They all looked at him with whitened eyes until the blond man realized it was a joke and started to laugh. Then the others joined in, with a chorus of bizarre-sounding chuckles and guffaws.

As predicted, Ramsey Clagg was in a poker game with four other men. They were seated on the ground around the edges of a tarpaulin. On one side of them was a small campfire. Illumination on the other side came from an acrid-smelling kerosene lantern with the wick turned up too high. Each man had a pile of coins in front of him. The cards, greasy and well worn, were tossed in the center of the canvas.

Remington surveyed the other players. He recognized three of them from wanted posters hanging in his office. The skinny one with the hand-rolled quirley hanging from his bottom lip was George Shoop, a small-time thief. Next to him was a fragile, gray-whiskered man named Doc Moorebridge. Remington remembered that the flier on him had listed sundry con games and forgery charges. Across from Clagg was a man called Lester Goodman, an ironic name, since the balding man was one of the most notorious horse thieves in the Nations. Remington did not know the fifth man. He was stocky, with shaggy brown hair, and kept his hand near the old Starr revolver stuck in the waistband of his pants. From the questioning gazes he cast at everyone else and the small pile of coins in front of him, he seemed to not know much about the art of poker.

"I've had enough for tonight," Doc Moorebridge announced, scooping up his change and funneling it into a pocket. "See you boys tomorrow."

"Mind if I sit in?" Remington asked Clagg.

"You got money? We don't play for matchsticks here, friend."

Remington nearly laughed in response. He had not seen any bills on the tarp, only coins. It was strictly a penny-ante game, the kind farmers and trailhands played for beer money.

"I think I can handle it."

"Then sit yourself down," Clagg said. "You got a name?"

"Remington."

For one heart-stopping moment Clagg looked curious, as though the name meant something to him. But then he laughed. "That's as good as any. As good as most of 'em here. I go by—"

"Ramsey Clagg."

"How'd *you* know?"

"You're a big man. You've got a big reputation."

Clagg visibly swelled with pride. It apparently mattered to him that others feared and respected him. That told Remington something about the red-haired man.

"It's five-card stud, Remington. Quarter limit. We're just havin' a friendly game here."

It dawned on the lawman that some of the money sitting in front of the buffalo hunter might belong to Elson O'Keefe. Remington did not have a plan yet, but he did need to do one important thing—win Clagg's confidence. It's easier to trap a varmint who thinks you're a friend. With that in mind, Remington offered Clagg a cigarette he had rolled earlier.

"Nah." Clagg waved the offering away. "I never smoke the stuff. I got enough other bad habits, right, boys?"

There was laughter all around at this comment, but Remington had filed away this bit of information. You never can tell what's important to remember about a man.

The talk died down once the game resumed. Remington found that the others were not very skilled at poker. He had little trouble accumulating four of the next six pots.

"You're a lucky man, Remington," Clagg commented.

"I've played my share of cards. A man picks up some experience if he pays attention."

The stocky man with the Starr revolver lost every hand. He made bonehead plays, scraped his cards on his chin every time he was dealt a decent hand. It did not take Remington long to pick up every player's "tell." Goodman gave a slight shrug to his shoulders. Shoop cleared his throat. And Clagg, when he got a good deal, had a barely noticeable tic at the corner of his left eye.

Remington's own face was impassive, his motions machine-like. He did the same thing after every deal, held his cards exactly the same way every time, kept any hint of expression from showing. The other players found him unreadable.

The stocky man was down to his last quarter when he cracked.

"Hey, you. Remington, ain't it? I think you're cheatin'."

"Friend, that's a dangerous accusation." The lawman's eyes were squinted, his hand ready. "You got something to back that up?"

"I got this!"

The man whipped his gun out.

Remington flipped his cards into the other man's face and swatted the barrel of the pistol aside. Once the marshal found his balance, he grabbed the muzzle of the revolver, twisting it until it jumped out of the man's hand. Remington tossed the weapon aside.

The shaggy-haired fellow lashed out with his left fist, cracking Remington on the side of the head. Bright spots danced in front of Remington's eyes. His hat sailed off into the darkness.

"Fight! Fight!" Ramsey Clagg shouted.

Men seemed to materialize out of the night. Within a minute they had Remington and the other cardplayer—Joe Beckart, somebody had called him—surrounded in a wide ring. The spectators began betting on the outcome. Most favored Beckart because he was stockier and appeared to be stronger. Those who had seen him fight before knew that eye-gouging, choking, and ear-boxing were some of his tricks when he could not win fairly.

Remington was faster than Beckart. He slipped some punches, bobbing his head left and right in a style the heavier man had never seen before.

Beckart was rattled by the shouts and catcalls of the crowd.

Remington ignored them. If he could win this fight, it would be a good opportunity for him. It could earn him these outlaws' grudging respect.

The stocky man could not keep pace with Remington's footwork. The marshal danced on the balls of his feet, shooting a jab out now and then, forcing Beckart into the kind of fight he was not accustomed to.

Finally the tension pushed Beckart into charging. He opened his thick arms, trying to get Remington into a bear hug. Remington leaped aside, but Beckart managed to grab him by the sleeve. Off balance, Beckart spun his adversary around so Remington's back was to him. In panic, he threw his arms around Remington, pinning his arms to his sides.

It was an awkward move. Remington guessed what might be coming next. Beckart would let go suddenly and slam his palms against his opponent's head, shattering his eardrums.

Remington squirmed his hands up as best he could. He got hold of Beckart's pinkie fingers and jerked outward.

Howling in pain, Beckart was forced to release his grip.

In that instant, Remington spun around, snatched the other man by the shirtfront, and began pummeling short, rapid-fire punches into Beckart's face. They did not have much power, but his arm was like a piston, shooting in and out, in and out, until Beckart's eyes rolled upward and his legs went slack. He was out.

Remington let the man drop. Beckart thudded to the ground like a felled tree.

For a while, Remington stood over him, panting. The crowd went silent. Maybe he had made a mistake. Maybe Beckart had been one of their favorites. Maybe now they were going to tear this stranger limb from limb.

He hung his hand away from his Colt. There were fifty, maybe seventy-five men ringed around him. It would be impossible to defend himself if shooting started.

The voice of Ramsey Clagg yelled from somewhere in the crowd, "Hell, the fun's over. C'mon, Remington! Let's get back to them cards."

Then, like a bunch of schoolboys, those tough, dangerous men let out a roaring cheer, signaling their approval of the stranger's victory. Those who had bet on Beckart and lost shook their heads. The few who had won collected their money and offered to buy drinks.

"Damn good fight," Clagg said, slapping Remington on the back with such force that it nearly knocked him off his feet. "Good, but too short. You shoulda played with Beckart more, Remington. I coulda won more money."

"You bet on me?"

"Sure. I seen your type before. A smart fighter. That knothead never stood a chance."

"Yeah," Remington conceded. He accepted the congratulations of some of the other men, as if he had just accomplished some worthwhile feat.

Within fifteen minutes, Remington, Clagg, Shoop, and Goodman had resumed their game. Remington noticed that his winnings—all of a dollar eighty-five—had been stolen while he was fighting, by Clagg, he presumed. He acted as if he did not notice. One fight a night was enough.

Most of the crowd had dispersed when one old man, balancing a rusty tin coffee cup in a shaky hand, stumbled over to the card game. He stood for several minutes, spilling more coffee than he sipped.

Clagg thought the man might be giving signals to one of the players. At last he lost his temper, barking out, "What the hell are you standing there for, you old fleabag?"

"I seen him before."

Remington had regained his hat and had it pulled down over his forehead. "Could be," he replied. "I've been in a lot of places."

"I seen him," the old man repeated to Clagg.

"So what?" pronounced the redheaded giant. He looked for something to throw. He did not want to make the effort to get up and go kick the old codger in the seat of the pants.

"It was . . . it was . . . yeah! It was in Missoura that I seen him," the old man stammered. He pointed a gnarled finger. "I seen him the the courtroom of that Hangin' Sam Barnstall. That there's a United States marshal!"

Chapter Eight

Remington did not stand around to argue.

He leaped up even as he saw Clagg about to clear leather. Remington put Lester Goodman, the horse thief, between himself and the big man's gun.

Clagg still triggered a shot, sending a forty-four-caliber ball from the massive Walker whizzing through a flapping part of Goodman's shirt.

With one quick blur of a motion, Remington swept his right boot into the campfire. The action was not meant to extinguish the flames but to spread them. The coals and burning logs sailed into the air.

Ramsey Clagg, still seated, caught a lapful. A red-hot ember as big as a fist flew inside George Shoop's shirtfront.

Then Remington grabbed the edge of the tarp with both hands and gave it a tremendous jerk. Men went rolling backward, sideways. Remington flipped the canvas up, tossing it on their heads.

He could hear screaming and cursing as he ran off into the night. Somewhere out there was his horse, tied to a small clump of bushes. He hoped he was running in the right direction.

Just when it looked as if he might get Clagg to fall for his story about running moonshine to the Indians and trick the buffalo hunter into leaving camp with him, the whole thing had fallen apart.

Remington knew he had been taking a big chance, riding into the middle of the outlaw camp as if he had never crossed paths with any of them. Most of the men he had brought back to Sam Barnstall's court either were still in prison or had been hanged.

But it had only taken that one old man to spot him.

"Hey! What the . . . ?"

Remington, nearly stumbling, looked down at the man rousting himself out of his bedroll. He had run right over him in the dark.

"Tryin' to steal my poke . . ." the man mumbled, fumbling under the wool blanket for his gun.

"Go back to sleep," Remington said, slamming a right cross into the fellow's chin. The outlaw collapsed in a heap.

At odd moments like these, when his life hung by a thread, Ned Remington wondered why he stayed a lawman. Farmers or freight haulers did not have people shooting at them in the pitch blackness, did they? Cowboys did not have a hundred men chasing them with the intent to roast them over a slow fire.

He cut a zigzag path, just as a precaution. The booming, cannonlike sound probably was coming from Ramsey Clagg's Sharps. The eruption of gunfire behind him sounded like a pack of yapping dogs.

Remington saw a heavy silhouette off to his right and made for it. He laughed aloud when he discovered that it was Shadow, exactly where he had left him.

Thank God he had not taken the saddle off yet. He snatched the reins, breaking the branch they were tied to instead of untying them. He pulled up on the cinch strap. Shadow sucked in air.

"C'mon, boy. No time for games now." He could hear the clattering of rocks as men approached.

The horse puffed out, the cinch came tight, and Remington made it fast. He swung into the saddle, never touching the stirrup.

The horse set out with no coaxing. He galloped off to the right. Remington could hardly see more than a dozen yards ahead of him, so it made little difference which way they went.

Back toward the camp, torches bobbed up and down like fireflies. Twisting in the saddle, Remington watched a string of them. He guessed the men were trying to find their horses and saddle up.

Clagg would be there, right at the head of them. Remington wasted no time berating himself for waltzing into this big hornets' nest. That would accomplish nothing. He put all of his attention on saving his skin.

He was sure that Hell's Door was not a box canyon, although he had not had the time to explore the nearby countryside. The outlaws would not choose a place where the army or Indians could bottle them up or even cut off another exit. Remington was willing to bet his life that there were more than two ways out of here.

On the way in he had seen no guards. That did not mean they were not there. But what would keep a man up on a lonely rim all night when there were cards and food and booze and women below? And even if he *did* stay up there, what would keep him from falling asleep?

Shadow picked out what looked like a trail. It could be a deer path, or just a narrow clearing free of shrubs and cactus. Remington had to chance it.

The horse walked along, snorting, putting his hooves down unsteadily. Remington knew that the other men might be familiar with the trails, but they had no way of telling where he was in this darkness.

Off in the distance came the sound of pursuing riders. They were not galloping. No one wanted to take a chance on injuring his horse in some stupid pitch-black manhunt.

"I think I see 'im, boys!" came Clagg's bellowing voice off the rocks.

Remington dismissed the ploy to force him to panic. He could not see Clagg, even with the camp behind them, so he was fairly sure the big outlaw could not see him. The marshal kept plugging ahead, slowly but definitely gaining ground.

A man loomed on a ridge!

Remington drew his Colt, sighted him. On closer inspection, it proved to be only an odd-shaped prickly pear. He eased the hammer back down on the lone empty chamber. He had come too close to giving himself away.

As Shadow plodded along, Remington turned in the saddle

to try to see the polestar. Where had it been when he had ridden into camp a few hours ago?

At last he located it and took a bearing. If the camp was off behind him and to his left, then he was going in the right general direction. He had noticed a small stream on the way in. That gurgling noise he heard might be it, or it might be another branch of it.

It might be noisy, but it seemed a safe bet. He decided to borrow a trick from the Comancheros he had followed into Hell's Door.

Shadow found the stream easily enough, and he stopped for a moment to slurp in it. Remington, in spite of his instinct to put his heels to him, let the horse take some water. It might be a long ride.

He urged the gelding up the stream, trying to keep him directly in the center of it. Remington was not trying to cover his tracks; it was dark and there was no need for that anyway. He was trying to pick the path of least resistance, and if this was the same creek he had noticed on the way into the camp, it would just as surely lead out.

It was not as noisy as he thought. The water was moving pretty quickly, bubbling and popping over the rocks and gravel in the streambed. Shadow's sloshing feet were hardly noticeable.

Scrub and brush crowded the sides at times, their branches closing in on top while their roots sought the life-giving water below. Remington pulled the leather cord over the front brim of his hat and tucked it under his chin so an errant branch would not knock the Stetson off.

Shouting echoed ahead.

Remington tugged back on the reins, stopping the mount. Shadow was superbly trained. Few horses could be made to walk up a swiftly flowing stream, and it was even tougher to do it at night. But these two had been together many years.

The gelding's breathing was slow and even. It could not be heard even a few feet from the stream. Remington did not move. He could not afford the squeaking of saddle leather, as much as he wanted to crouch down.

The locust trees and bushes fronting the creek broke up

Remington's silhouette. His hand went down to his gun again when he saw a dancing torch, but it disappeared just as quickly as its owner trotted his horse down into a gully.

The marshal figured he was getting close to the canyon's mouth. Staying off the trail and keeping to this stream had turned into a stroke of genius.

Until his luck ran out.

The horse stopped by itself. Wary, Remington leaned out as far as he dared and saw the reason. A dead tree had fallen across the stream, its spiky branches sticking out like the spines of a porcupine. The water was flowing under it.

Reluctantly he pulled the reins to his left and eased the horse onto dry ground. For a moment it stood motionless, wondering what it was supposed to do next. Remington wondered the same thing.

If Clagg had any brains at all, he would have headed for the entrance to the canyon, figuring Remington would have *had* to come in that way, since, being a lawman, he was unfamiliar with the land. Odds were that big man was even now camped behind a boulder or a tree, his Sharps ready. Remington intended to disappoint him.

One reason the marshal had managed to stay alive so long was that he was brilliant at putting himself inside another man's head. He could think so much like an outlaw that he sometimes wondered why he had not become one. But he knew. Deep down inside, he knew.

Clagg would take the canyon pass himself. He would order all torches put out. He would station a few men, in a fan pattern, before the mouth of the gorge, and several on the other side of it, just in case Remington somehow managed to slip by. He would position the men so that their stray shots would not hit one another and would warn them to keep absolutely silent so he could hear the lawman approaching.

That was why Remington went in the opposite direction.

It meant crossing the stream again, something the horse did not mind. He eased through a thicket of locusts. Remington was thankful that a light breeze was blowing, stirring the raspy leaves. Any noise would help his cover.

Somebody knocked a tin can down a hill. As it rattled off

the rocks a low voice cursed; then, realizing he was giving away his position even more clearly, the man went silent. Remington steered clear of the area.

The thin slice of moon provided just enough illumination before a wispy curtain of clouds slid across it. Remington saw what he needed to.

Ahead of him lay another way out of the canyon, a way the outlaws were not guarding, but it was probably left open because they thought it was impassable.

From where he sat on his horse to the rim of the canyon was a steep hill, composed of loose dirt, gravel, and steer-sized boulders. It would be like trying to walk up a steeply pitched roof in hard-soled shoes.

Remington considered his options, deciding that he had none. He knew that Clagg lay waiting along the entrance trail. Probably he had sent some men to cover the other exits, just in case. This impossible slide was still preferable to riding into an ambush.

The marshal had seen the gelding perform miracles, but this seemed insurmountable. Besides the sharp angle, the dirt and small stones would provide treacherous footing at best.

Remington thought it wisest to dismount and try to lead the animal up. No sense forcing it to balance him as well as itself.

The marshal stepped out ahead, the reins in one hand and the Henry rifle in the other for balance. Shadow followed gamely. He would go wherever this man led him.

They made good progress for fifty or seventy-five feet; then the dirt turned to gravel, interspersed with rounded, egg-sized stones. Remington's boots went out from under him and he went facedown, barely catching himself in time.

He paused for a moment, listening. By now the gelding was breathing harder, blowing every so often, but there were no sounds of pursuing riders. So far they had not been detected.

Remington continued the ascent. His shoulder ached from breaking his fall, but it was far better than a smashed nose. The horse dug in with his powerful haunches, propelling himself forward in little jumps, then pulling himself up with his front hooves. Remington was scrambling with his boots perpendicular to the slope, cutting a solid foothold with each step.

The lawman took a look above them. They were nearly at the halfway mark. Even in the darkness, the rim of the canyon was faintly visible.

Just then the gelding completed one of his short jumps, but his front hooves found only stones instead of dirt and gravel. The black's back legs floundered. He sidestepped, trying to right himself.

Remington yanked on the reins. The mount turned his head, then whipped it back. By then he was unable to regain his balance.

Shadow went down on his flanks. As Remington saw the horse's legs go up in the air, he knew the situation was out of his control. He held on to the reins, though. He could not let the animal go down alone.

What happened next was a testament to the black horse's remarkable agility. As he slid, rolled, twisted on his back, he kicked out with his legs until he was off his back and onto his side.

Then his left front leg was stabbing out, grabbing solid ground. The right leg found a foothold. He set his haunches. Slowly, very slowly, he righted himself, then stood up.

Remington could barely believe what he had seen. The horse appeared uninjured. It snorted twice and coughed, then gingerly started walking over to him.

"Easy, boy," he said to the black, patting it gently on the neck to calm it. "We'll get out of this yet."

They continued the climb, more slowly now. Remington steered them around the slippery patch of rocks. The horse lost its footing again but caught itself before it was in danger of falling over.

They were two-thirds of the way up the hill when the mask of clouds slipped off the moon.

The clattering rocks cascading down the slope caught the ear of a lone rider somewhere below.

"Hey!" he yelled upward. "Who is it? Who's makin' that noise?"

Remington hoped the man would think it was just another outlaw fumbling around in the dark on Clagg's crazy order.

A large-bore rifle boomed in the distance. The ball whined off a boulder, sending a shower of chips Remington's way. He looked up at the moon, looked down the slope, looked up at the rim. He was out in the open. With the clouds gone, they could see him well enough to adjust after a few shots and find the range.

"Who you shootin' at?" a second gruff voice demanded.

"That marshal! I got him pinned down up on that hill. Go get Clagg!"

Within minutes, a dozen of them would be sniping at him. Remington wanted to move again, but he did not want to expose his back to that rifleman. Instead, he crouched on one knee a few yards from the horse, raised the Henry, and levered off four rapid shots.

The outlaw was using the trees and brush behind him for a screen. Remington could not see him. He waited. Another shot came, the bullet whizzing only a foot over his head.

But Remington had pinpointed the muzzle flash. From the sound of the gun, the man was probably using a rolling-back breechloader or a paper-cartridge gun.

Remington aimed in the general direction and triggered off three quick shots, about a foot apart. Even up near the top of the hill, he could hear the horse squeal.

The man had had enough time to reload, but no more shots came. The lawman did not know what had happened, but he was not going to stay around to find out.

"C'mon, Shadow. Let's get the hell out of here."

As soon as the dark figure took the reins in his hand again, the horse knew what to do. He resumed his wild but effective series of jumps and lurches, eating up ground, Remington by his side struggling to keep up.

More shots came, now like a string of firecrackers. The ground seemed to pop and erupt around them. Dirt exploded into the air, rocks and pebbles became vicious projectiles.

Remington dared a few more rounds from the Henry. He heard a man scream far below. Clagg's thundering voice was roaring out something as well, but Remington could not understand it.

There, two dozen feet away, a head stuck up over the rim of the canyon!

Remington let the Henry fall and snatched the Colt out of his holster. The gun swept up and fired even as the head was ducking down. Then the man appeared, a rifle in his arms. Remington shot him, once, twice more, but the first bullet had done it. Staggering a few feet, the outlaw stumbled over the canyon rim, crashing down the rocky slope, end over end, a lifeless hulk.

The shots from Clagg and his bunch were getting closer. The bullets and minié balls whined overhead, like the tiny harbingers of death that they indeed were.

Remington spotted the rim. For its entire length, it was like a steep shelf, a cliff twenty feet high that ended at the slope he was climbing.

He saw a break in it, a ten-foot-wide gorge cracked and eroded away. It was the only place he could get the horse through.

The outlaws fired like there was no tomorrow. It was sheer chance that they had not hit Shadow.

Then, as quickly as his luck had gone sour back at the card game, Remington's fortunes turned again.

A smudge of clouds drifted across the moon.

The dim glow was wiped out. Looking up, Remington saw that his chance would last only thirty seconds or so. He jumped into the saddle now, slapping his boots to the horse and guiding him toward the opening.

The gunfire behind him crackled again.

As the moon once more peeked out the gang down by the trees adjusted their sights.

But it was too late. The dark rider was gone.

Chapter Nine

Remington wanted to rest his horse, but he knew that now was not the time for it.

Once the gelding got over the rim of the canyon, he did not slow down until his rider tugged back on the reins. The mount's sense of urgency was strange. Remington knew the horse had not been overly frightened by the gunfire. They had been shot at before, and Shadow had behaved admirably.

For *his* part, the marshal was glad to be gone from the shooting gallery of a slope, yet regretful that he had lost his chance to lure Ramsey Clagg away from the outlaw haven with his tale of selling moonshine to the Indians.

Remington stopped for a moment to think. There was no way that he could return to Hell's Door. If he let himself be captured by the outlaws, it would be suicide.

A half-dozen schemes flitted through his head, but he rejected all of them. He could not hope to approach the redheaded man face to face again. Clagg wanted his hide.

That was it!

Looking behind him, Remington managed to pick out a few trees and some large boulders. Most of the landscape was lost in the darkness. From far below came muted noises, but they were so faint that he could make no sense of them.

The lawman realized that Clagg still wanted him. Remington could easily escape now. He had enough of a lead on them. If he rode Shadow as fast as he dared through this blackness, he might be able to cover his trail out the same way the outlaws had disguised their trails on the way in.

But Ned Remington was not going to do that. He was

going to play the most dangerous game, the one in which the hunted turns and becomes the hunter. Even though he had managed to elude the killer, Remington understood that Clagg was no idiot. Far from it.

The marshal had to make Clagg follow him. It would mean letting the big man get tantalizingly close, only to slip out of his clutches so he would be enraged enough to keep up the chase. Remington was aware that if Clagg caught up and overtook him, the odds might be dozens against one.

Remington meant to whittle down those odds considerably. If they came after him—and he was counting that they would —they would travel in a group, safe because of their number, or so they would think.

The plan was still fuzzy yet. Remington did not know how he would cut them off. Yet it was the best idea he could come up with.

After several minutes, the sound from the distance grew louder. Remington put a cause to it. The outlaw band had backtracked through the darkness from the creekbank to the mouth of the canyon. None of them wanted to attempt the treacherous, rocky slope. Maybe they thought Remington would be waiting for them at the top of the rise with the deadly Henry rifle.

He tried to lay out the country in his mind's eye. Toward the canyon entrance, where they would emerge, were ravines and washes, generally hilly terrain. Ahead of him were—he thought—ridges and winding trails.

He had paid attention to the landmarks and odd-shaped trees on the way in, but they did him little good in the dark. Remington consulted his pocket watch. Just enough glow came down from the thin moon to read it. He figured a couple more hours till dawn.

First light would put him at the disadvantage. The Henry had good range and could rattle off a dozen or more shots without reloading, but Ramsey Clagg was a buff'ler, and expert at shooting at incredible distances. Remington's back would be too tempting a target for the man's Sharps.

Then the marshal reconsidered. That was not the way it would go. Shooting from a distance at a riding man was always tricky. Even the finest marksman could not allow for the oddities of a horse's gait or a man's sudden movement or any of a dozen other factors.

What Ramsey Clagg would want to do, in Remington's calculation, was wound him. Knock him out of the saddle. That would leave him alive for the sport. This man who had caused a slow and agonizing death to a sheriff's deputy would take an even greater delight in inflicting such a torture on a chief territorial marshal, especially one who had come to arrest him.

That alone would keep Clagg on the track.

The lawman was on high ground. Far below he could hear men leaving the pass for more open country. Despite their attempts to keep quiet, there was the inevitable creaking of leather, coughing, and clopping of horses' hooves.

Remington slid his long gun out of its boot. As he cocked it the horse automatically lowered his head. Remington let go a shot toward the gang.

The report echoed and reverberated off the trees and cliff faces, making it sound like five guns instead of one. The bullet ricocheted somewhere below with a murderous screech.

The single shot caused panic. Horses whinnied, men swore and shouted at one another. A few even triggered off responses before Clagg's distinctive voice squawked out over the din.

"Hold your fire, you dumb bastards! Can't you see he's tryin' to spook us?"

"Yuh think that's him?"

"Who the hell else would it be?" Clagg snapped back. "He didn't get as far as we thought. Maybe his horse come up lame in that climb. Anybody see where that shot come from?"

"I can't see nothin'," one of the group complained. "I don't like ridin' around in the dark like this, Clagg. Who knows when that fool's gonna throw off another shot at us, and the next one might hit *me.* "

"You headin' back?"

There was silence. Remington judged that the man was more afraid of big Ramsey Clagg than he was of stray gunfire in the middle of the night.

"Anybody else?" Clagg demanded.

Silence again.

"Then let's get after the son of a bitch. And remember, we have to take him alive. Any one of you that kills him'll have to answer to me."

Well, Remington decided, their purposes were the same. Each of them wanted to take the other alive. But the lawman knew *he* could hardly do it with twenty or thirty other outlaws around. Right at the moment, Clagg had intimidated them all into sticking with him.

Remington vowed to change that.

He listened to them picking their way along the trails. From the sounds that drifted up, they seemed to be going slower, more cautiously.

The marshal sat up on the rise as long as he thought sensible.

"How do we know that Remington fella didn't just get that one shot off at us, then hightail it back for where he come from?" one of the men whined.

"We *don't* know it," Clagg snapped. "But it'll be light soon, and no matter how fast he's goin', he won't have time to cover his trail."

The marshal walked his horse off the vantage point and down a small hillock. Clagg had a point. Soon it *would* be dawn. Remington knew he could keep out in front of them; he was confident of the gelding's stamina.

Suddenly it hit the lawman, turning his stomach into a tight, twisted knot. What if Clagg, the expert buffalo hunter, sighted in with his long-barreled Sharps and put a ball into Shadow?

Remington could not escape on foot. He could prolong the hunt, but the outcome would be inevitable.

He was not sure of the range of the big guns the bandits carried. It made his situation ever trickier. He had to stay on the fringe—just far enough out that they could not make an accurate, or even lucky, shot, but still where they could see him.

Remington's instincts told him to conserve his ammunition, but he drew the Henry out of its sleeve and blasted a shot—straight into the air.

At least four shots, maybe five, answered back. Clagg might have iron nerves, but the men with him were as tightly wound as a fifty-cent watch. Even on the other side of the ridge, Remington could hear them cursing one another as their jumpy horses bumped into the next rider. Loudest was Clagg's voice, its gravelly pitch strained almost to a screech.

"You stupid jackasses!" he yelled. "That time he wasn't even shootin' at us. Didn't you hear the way that shot died away instead of echoin'? Now keep them damn guns in your holsters. He's got you all spooked."

Remington was chipping at them, wearing their resolve away. Not long and it would be light. His element of surprise would be gone. These outlaws would calm down when they could see where they were and that they were no longer in danger.

The marshal wondered just how long the gang would tag along with Clagg. Fear held them now, but if they began to desert, there was probably little he could do about it. It would not inspire confidence in the loyal ones if the traitors got shot.

Remington hefted his canteen. Fortunately, it was full. He would have no chance to stop for water in the coming day, even if he could find some. Maybe Clagg would even send out some fast-riding scouts to wait at all the nearby water holes. The marshal hoped that Shadow would be able to hold out on the drink he had taken back at the stream. With the coming heat and a hard ride, the horse would lose a lot of water.

"C'mon, Shadow, let's do some riding." He slipped the long gun back in its holster, giving the horse a light thump with his heels.

They uncovered a trail and were a quarter mile along it before Remington recognized that it was getting light. The first pink rays gave him a direction to ride toward—east, and a little south, back toward the Texas Panhandle.

How far away was it? He could only guess a couple days, and hope that just Clagg was following him by the time they reached it. If the other men did not lose interest or did not decide they would be safer back in the brigands' hideout, then Remington would give them a little convincing along the way.

The irony of the situation did not escape him. Now *he* was being chased, instead of doing the chasing. He was still in control; they were not gaining on him. Yet he began to understand how a fugitive might feel. The mob behind him might just as well have been a posse or an enraged bunch of vigilantes.

Remington thought every runaway was probably convinced that *he* was somehow different, that *he* could escape, that *he* would never hear that iron door clang shut or feel that trap drop beneath his feet, then jerk him into oblivion.

A bead of sweat dribbled down the lawman's forehead, alongside his nose, and lost itself in his black, bushy mustache. What if he were wrong now?

He shook the thought out of his head and lost himself in the horse's easy canter. Up and down he went until he was no longer thinking, until he was hypnotized by the flowing rhythm.

A shot whipped him out of his reverie. It sliced overhead; he could not place where.

He swiveled in the saddle. The Hell's Door bunch was breaking through a small stand of trees. The men and horses were far enough away and the light was still faint enough that they were only black specks.

Their shouting was barely audible. Remington guessed that Clagg had attempted a shot at his horse, or maybe one of the others had and the big man had berated him because it was too tricky at such a distance. Clagg would not have been concerned about the fellow's missing. He would be angry because the bullet might have killed the dark rider.

Something was wrong. Remington sensed that the situation was quickly turning even more dangerous.

He looked behind him again. Then, straining his eyes, watching the many-limbed specks, he saw that they were riding hard, *very* hard.

Now that they could see him, they intended to run him down and put an end to this game in a hurry.

"Run! Run!" he commanded the horse.

The change was not instantaneous, but Remington knew enough about the gelding's ways. Gradually the black went from a rolling canter to a full gallop, then to a muscle-straining run. Ground disappeared behind them as if it were on fire.

Remington gave the gelding his head for four or five minutes before he slowly applied some pressure with his knees. Just as smoothly as he had put on the burst of speed, the horse eased back into a sprightly canter again.

A check behind told the marshal that the bandits had turned into even tinier specks. They would not be able to push their horses that hard indefinitely if they wanted to continue the chase.

As the sun nudged its way over the horizon, Remington scanned the countryside. Somewhere back near Hell's Door, when it was dark, in unfamiliar territory, he had taken a different turn from the way he had come in. He was on a small mesa which was quickly dropping off to lower terrain.

The table rock gave him a good view of the land before him. He liked what he saw. He was coming out of the mountains into a maze of foothills. Somewhere out there was the Canadian River and, south of it, Amarillo.

His thoughts drifted to the waitress in that café where he had eaten breakfast. It seemed a hundred years ago. He promised himself he would make some time for her after he slammed the door on Clagg in the Amarillo jail.

Through the rest of the day, the terrain favored Remington. The trails and clearings wound back and forth so that the lawman had no trouble staying far ahead of the gang while at the same time not letting himself stumble into their rifle sights.

It was an intricate contest, but Remington played it well. As much as he could, he conserved Shadow's strength. Once they broke into flat, open country, he would need every bit of distance that the horse could give him.

It was a dangerous act, yet Remington paused at water holes and creeks as often as he could. He was painfully aware that his survival in the next few days depended entirely on having a superbly conditioned animal under him.

They wound down, down, to the lower elevations. Rem-

ington could not notice that the air was less thin, but his horse
seemed to appreciate it. These snarls of gullies and ravines
and meandering hills would last all the next day, Remington
thought. He brought out the tattered map again and was surprised to see that they might be swinging within a few hours
of the farm of Elson O'Keefe, where Remington had dropped
off his badge.

The marshal was surprised at Clagg's patience. He had half
expected the lot of them to turn back long before now. Not
enough of them had turned chicken and run. Remington swore
to decrease their numbers himself.

All through the late afternoon and early evening he con-
cocted his plan. Would it be possible to make some of the
outlaws desert at night?

Remington was hoping that, even though these men were
as tough as any to be found in the West, they were not accustomed to working for a living. These were men who believed
in stealing and raping as a way of life, men who did not have
the courage or the fortitude to put their backs to daily labor.
They had rebelled against the rules all their lives, and the
lawman was figuring that they would do it again.

Torturing a U.S. marshal might be great sport, but Remington aimed to make it more trouble than it would be worth
for them. More important, he intended to rattle their nerves
and give them enough of a scare that following Clagg and
going on would be more dangerous than turning back.

Every few hours, Remington would become aware that
they were following him. Out ahead, he could occasionally
hear the mumbling echo of their voices, even though the
sounds were too indistinct to understand. They understood the
situation too. As long as they were in this twisting, rugged
country, they were fairly safe. They could not see the lawman, but he could not see them, either.

Remington made a meal of jerky and crackers, eating as he
rode, washing it down with water from his canteen. The meat
was so hardened and tough that it made his jaw ache just
chewing it enough to swallow it. Still, it had a certain salty,
invigorating taste to it, quieting the growling in his belly and
renewing his strength.

It reminded him of the hundreds of other meals he had eaten in the saddle. Those times he had been in pursuit, or hell-bent to make a town before a train or a riverboat pulled out. Being a lawman meant being able to adapt, to subject your body to all kinds of stresses and strains. Above all, it meant keeping a clear head no matter how you felt or what was happening around you.

Nightfall huddled down slowly across the hills. It began with the dimness that made the ground harder to follow, until finally he was riding in total darkness, lucky to keep branches out of his face.

Remington realized they were no longer pursuing him. They had camped for the night.

What Clagg had done made sense. They were skilled enough trackers that Remington could not elude them. And it would be stupid of him to try to ride all night to gain ground on them. All he would do was tire his horse and himself so that they would easily be able to catch up and overtake him the next day.

Remington rode another fifteen or twenty minutes until he located a campsite he liked. It was not out in front of where he supposed the outlaws were, but more parallel to them. If they sent scouts ahead looking for him, at least he would not be where they expected.

Shadow munched the thick grass, oblivious of the darkness. After he had laid out the phony bedroll and had something more to eat, Remington decided that it was time to enact his plan.

He followed his ears to their camp. Clagg was wise enough to order the men not to build fires, but he allowed them to talk. He must have figured a lone, bone-weary marshal would not be foolhardy enough to attack a group that outnumbered him twenty to one.

On that notion, Ramsey Clagg was wrong.

Remington crept in with all the stealth of a big mountain cat. The soundless way he glided through the night was uncanny, yet it had come only after years of practice and learning the tricks of the Cheyenne and the Kiowa.

He moved in, downwind of their horses, crawling up a

little mound until he could overlook their camp. This was one of those times when his black clothing proved practical. He had darkened his face with a lump of charcoal he kept in his saddlebag for just that purpose. Hat pulled low on his head, he propped himself up on one elbow and looked down at the men. Several of them had already climbed into their bedrolls, their raucous snoring sounding like a platoon of lumberjacks.

Remington tried to count them, but it was a waste of time. Their dark wool blankets, coupled with the distance and lack of light, made them almost blend into the ground. He was surprised at their number. Clagg must have inspired plenty of respect or fear or both to get so many mavericks to follow him on such a risky quest.

"We'll break out just before dawn," Clagg was telling a group of other men. "Them that wants can build fires then, heat up beans or fry bacon, but we ain't gonna dawdle around here long. Likely Remington'll be tryin' to widen the gap between us tomorrow."

"Think he'll head for a fort?" a lanky man asked.

"I think we'll catch up to him afore then," Clagg returned in a tone of self-confidence. "Hell, that black of his may be good, but it can't run forever. Sooner or later the bastard'll go out, then we'll have him."

"Yeah," voiced another. "So long as he ain't in Amarillo before that happens."

"You fellas worry too much," Clagg said. "You're like a bunch of old women, you know that?"

"Well," snorted the tall man, in an attempt at a joke, "if anybody'd know about old women, it'd be you, Clagg."

"I'll clue you somethin', boys, the last woman I had wasn't old. And she was a hell of a fighter. Farm woman, up in these hills. Not too far from here, I expect. Just 'fore I rode into Hell's Door."

Then he proceeded with a detailed account of his rape of Sarah O'Keefe, laughing every few sentences, slapping the others on their backs, describing it as if it were the same as breaking a bronco.

Remington had to restrain himself from taking the Colt and doing away with Clagg right then and there. But he had made a solemn promise to Judge Sam Barnstall and even to Elson O'Keefe. That kind of swift retribution, a shot in the night, would not be justice.

But it sure as hell would feel good.

Creeping about the perimeter of the camp, listening to the conversations, Remington picked up the identities of several of the outlaw gang members. Most of them were murderers or robbers or were wanted for some other capital crime.

Clagg was the only one he had a warrant for. He would lose no sleep doing what he had to do to the others to bring the big man in. Remington was only too aware that it was their lives or his.

When he crept up behind the guard at the remuda, he had no second thoughts about using his knife on him.

The outlaw went down without a sound, just as Remington wanted. If he had tried to buffalo him with his pistol barrel, he might have given him a glancing blow, allowing him to shoot or even groan. The success of his plan hinged on silence.

Clagg was too confident. The man guarding the string of horses was the only sentry Remington encountered. The redhead must have thought Remington would be too weary or too scared to try any after-dark maneuvers.

The men were sleeping in a sort of basin. Around it were low hills or rises. Here and there was a tree, but it was mostly clear, open. Perfect for what Remington had in mind.

The horses went with him almost dumbly. They were too tired to give any protest. When he had them in position, Remington put the Henry to his shoulder and fired into the ground. He cranked off a half-dozen shots, blasting away near the horses' hooves.

The stampede swept right down through the camp, as the marshal had schemed.

Men in bedrolls awoke too late to get out of the way of the onrushing mounts. Remington thought none of them would be killed—there were not enough horses for that—but they would certainly be too hurt and sore to go on with the chase.

He did enough shouting and shooting to sound like a tribe

of Apaches, and it was several seconds before some of the men realized that it was not.

Some of the outlaws returned fire into the night, wasting their bullets but venting their rage. The rush of horses was gone as quickly as it had come, but it did its damage.

Ramsey Clagg, hand clapped to a bleeding forehead, screamed at the top of his voice, "Goddam you, Remington! I'm gonna kill you slow and hard. *Real* hard!"

Chapter Ten

As exhausted as he was, Remington should have fallen into a dreamless slumber, but that was not the case at all. After returning from his solo raid, he got into his bedroll—hidden from the rest of his camp—and struggled through hours of fitful sleep, laced with haunting nightmares.

He imagined that he was caught in a sort of lawman's hell, the object of this damnable chase through the rest of eternity. Every so often a ghostly outlaw band would catch up to him, torture him with hot pitchforks and irons; then he would escape, only to be chased again.

Remington drifted in and out of sleep. A cold sweat had formed on his forehead. At first, he was not sure whether he was still dreaming or awake. He thought he heard a sound. Maybe it was only in his mind.

He was about to let himself slip away when he heard it again. This was not a dream. Someone had come for him.

Slowly, very carefully, he found his pocket watch and held it up near his face. Four, maybe five hours had passed since he had killed that guard and stampeded the outlaws' horses.

It made sense. The ones who could travel were done nursing their wounds. Clagg must have sent out some scouts to look for him, just as Remington had guessed he might.

The marshal thought before he moved. He could simply lie there, waiting for the intruder to come to him, but that gave the outlaw a better chance of getting the drop on him.

Remington peeled back his blanket. The old, thick wool made no sound, not even the slightest rustling. He got up on one elbow and looked around him.

It was still dark. Judging from the time, he reckoned he had at least an hour before dawn.

The man creeping around his camp was good, but not good enough. He would have been quiet enough to take an ordinary man. Not only was Remington a light sleeper, he had taken the precaution of scattering dry twigs and leaves about. To his sensitive ear, they were as effective as an alarm bell.

Remington got out of his blanket and onto his feet. He did not want to move around too much at first. The twigs could give him away too.

He let his eyes get adjusted to the dark. A black shape became a tree; that bulky object off to his left was his horse.

Leaning over the phony bedroll was the stranger.

Remington could see well enough to tell that the man had his pistol drawn, aimed down where the sleeper's head should be. He was smart enough to stand away near the top, so the sleeping man, if he had a gun concealed under the blanket, would have to shoot upside down to get him.

The marshal assumed the outlaw wanted to take him alive. That would have been Clagg's orders. Of course, the man could always claim that he had fired defending himself, that he had had no other choice. After the stampede, that was how it would probably go.

Remington did not intend to let the other man fire. The shot might draw other scouts, or even the big buffalo hunter himself.

With one swift motion, the outlaw whipped the blanket off, cocked his pistol, and jammed it down to where he thought Remington's head was.

"Hey!" Remington said.

The bandit turned, raising his gun as he did.

All he saw was a furtive motion in the dark. The next thing he knew, a leather-handled throwing knife seemed to have sprouted from his chest.

He tried to scream, to warn the others, but it was impossible. He was dead before he hit the ground.

Remington ran over and collected the knife, wiping the blood off on the ground. He returned it to its secret sheath down his back. He checked the man's pulse, just to be sure. There was none.

"Shadow! You ready to go, boy?" he whispered.

The horse danced around a little, shaking itself out of its much-deserved sleep. Remington gathered up his gear quickly.

The thin shaving of a moon that had favored him the night before was hovering near the horizon, providing enough of a glow for Remington to extract a scrap of paper and a stub of a pencil from his saddlebag. He did the printing mostly by touch. the moon did not give off enough light to see it. The letters and lines would run together, but it would be legible.

He found a small rock, put the letter on the dead man's bloody chest, then weighted it down.

A few minutes later he was mounted and walking his horse down a grassy hill. Fairly sure he was clear of any other outlaw scouts, he talked to the gelding in a low, friendly voice, patting it on the neck every now and then.

Remington had a strange way of thinking about this horse. He knew that it would obey his commands, would follow his signals, but any horse could be taught to do that. What made Shadow different was that he would go on when other animals might stop. He would run faster and harder when that extra burst of speed could mean the difference between life and death. Maybe Remington only imagined the reason, but he thought not. He felt the big black did it out of a sense of *loyalty.*

The lawman remembered the note he had left. They would eventually pick up the trail and would find their dead companion. Remington could almost see the big man's reaction.

Clagg, the note read, *you've got a funny way of taking care of your friends. Looks like you've finally met your match. Tell your friends if they stick with you, I've got more surprises for them. Remington.*

If he had him figured right—and Remington thought he did by now—Clagg would read the note, or have somebody read it to him; then he would stare out into space for a while. His face would become red as his anger boiled inside him. Then he would snatch the note, tear it into pieces, throw them on the ground, and roar to his men to get saddled up and ready to ride.

Either way, the note would have an effect. If Clagg were unable to read and had to have someone else read it out loud, the rest of the gang would hear, especially the part about more surprises. Even if Clagg read it to himself, it would incite him, drive him ever farther into the chase.

Remington realized there was a degree of danger in such taunting. But he had come too far now. If Clagg caught him, what more could he do to him because of the note?

The lawman had no intention of letting the redheaded killer catch him, though. Farther, farther east he was leading them, out of their thieves' haven of hills into spreading, flat land. He might get some help from a passing cavalry troop.

Then it struck him that he had no way of identifying himself to others as a lawman. If the troopers did not recognize any of them, Clagg might even claim that *they* were a group of vigilantes and that *Remington* was an escaped killer.

He dismissed that thought quickly. It would do him no good to let it rattle around inside his head. It was a possibility, true, but he would confront it, if he had to, when the time came.

The horse had eased into that rolling canter that it could maintain for hours. Remington glanced behind him but caught no sign of his pursuers. They were probably gathered around their comrade's body, watching Clagg go into his little rage, wondering what the hell they were doing out here.

By tonight, Remington wanted to give them so many doubts that turning back would seem the only sane alternative. He wanted to come up with a plan, another raid, but he knew that they would be better prepared next time they camped. They would post guards. Maybe they would even come out looking for him. Clagg would not make the same mistake twice.

Remington reached behind him in his saddlebags and drew out his bag of grub. He was sorely aware that he would have to ration it; there was no telling how long this might go on. But from yesterday's long ride and the restless sleep, he was light-headed. A meal right now was vital.

First he ate a few crackers to get his juices going. Then he took a drink of water, following it with a bite of jerky.

He tried to remember the last time he had had a cup of coffee; then he recalled the meal he had wolfed down at the crude eat place in Hell's Door. He had to laugh. Even *that* rough fare would go good right now. He thought of the fine breakfast he had shared with the farmer, Elson O'Keefe. O'Keefe was probably getting up about now, turning to his chores, wondering why he was carrying on with his wife gone.

Then Remington thought of the waitress in the Amarillo café. Something about her had told him that she did not take an interest in every male customer she happened to serve. He wondered why he could not get her out of his head. Maybe it was her green eyes or that pretty bucktoothed smile of hers.

O'Keefe must have felt that way about his Sarah when they first met, Remington thought. There must have been that bolt of lightning that she was different, that she was special, that she just might be the one for him. Obviously the man had still been completely fascinated by her right up to the moment she died.

Suddenly Remington became very angry. No man had a right to do what Clagg had done and get away with it. Judge Barnstall was right. A bullet was too good for a man like that. A bullet was too fast, too merciful.

When a man comes upon the greatest treasure he could find in a lifetime, no one has the right to steal it away from him. The same held true for Pete Trask's widow. From what Remington had learned, Trask had been a good man, a family man.

These outrages demanded justice—Sam Barnstall's kind of justice. Remington knew that he and his deputies were only a few, but they had to see that men like Clagg were punished for these crimes so that others would think twice—or three times —before they cased a bank or raided a farm or pulled a knife on somebody.

The food and the anger had snapped the marshal back to reality. His thinking cleared up. He felt strength returning to him.

The sun was already over the horizon, casting an orange aura across the sky in the east. Remington watched a flock of crows flapping and wheeling overhead, cawing at him for invading their territory so early in the day.

He dug in his saddlebags and pulled out the brass spyglass. Pulling it open, he scrutinized the range behind him.

What looked like a tiny swirl of dust from the wind was actually the cloud behind Clagg and his riders. Remington took the time to count. As best he could tell at this distance, their ranks had fallen to about ten. That was half the number that had been chasing him yesterday. The stampede had done the trick. He wondered how many of *these* men were injured and would want to quit after a day's hard riding.

Remington stood there, looking through the telescope, longer than he should have. For some reason, he wanted to see these men, he wanted to know who he was up against. It did not take long to put names to the faces.

On the outside of the string was Fitz Durrant, an Arkansan wanted in a half-dozen states for crimes ranging from horse theft to assault. Next to him and a little back was Isham Hyatt, a certified crazy man out of the John Brown mold who believed it was his ordained duty to rid the West of all evildoers. His problem was that he had no idea what evil really was, and he killed—indiscriminately—anyone who fit his warped notion.

Two of the men the marshal did not know. It could be they were from California; Remington did not get many posters from that part of the country. Then there was Rudy Sumter, a half-witted, sadistic former guard from Andersonville Prison who had somehow eluded the military courts and had been dodging the law ever since. Remington noticed the Ballard brothers, Joe and Emmett, who had formed a gang of their own a few years back, causing general havoc in Missouri and Iowa until Sam Barnstall took office and they moved west.

When he took the glass down, they were closer than he had thought. Dangerously close. Close enough to take a shot at his horse and get lucky.

Remington folded the telescope shut and jammed it inside his shirt. With a grab and a swing, he was in the saddle, wheeling the big black and thumping bootheels into his flanks.

What had fooled Remington was that Clagg and his band were riding hard, unusually hard, probably trying to overtake him as they had tried the day before. Maybe they thought they could finish it early. Maybe they thought the lawman or his mount had not had sufficient rest last night. Or maybe they were just frustrated as hell and wanted to put a quick end to it.

The land was still hilly enough that he could follow one of these winding gulches and make it away from them. He knew they could not push their horses like that for long. They were taking the risk of tiring them for the rest of the day.

He angled downward, walking the black across a steep ravine. They took their time until they were in the bottom of it, beside a sluggish stream; then Remington urged the horse to trot again.

By the time Clagg and the others got there, they would find only tracks. Remington was counting that the big man would slow down to spell their horses. They might even stop beside the stream to water them, but if they did that, they would need some time to cool them.

Remington kept riding, concentrating on widening the gap. He was no longer worried that they would throw it in and give up on him. It had turned into a blood feud for them now.

The other men, those crazies he had seen through the glass, were like a pack of mad dogs. If they ever caught up to him, they would tear him limb from limb, snarling and growling and snapping at one another.

Now he did not have to worry about riding too fast for them.

The scruffy grass and shrubs gave way to yellow paloverde and mesquite, affording him cover of a fashion. At least he could ride between the clumps of trees and not feel as exposed as a fly on a whitewashed wall. As the morning wore on and the sun began to climb, Remington became aware of the dry heat and the wind blowing in from the plains far below.

He knew what he had to do, but his lawman's code rebelled against it. It was the only way to come out of this alive. It seemed a cowardly thing, but after hours of arguing with himself, he finally decided to do it.

He had to lay an ambush.

There was no other way. It was an outlaw's tactic, but after all, he was fighting outlaws, and this was hardly the time to be a gentleman.

All the scruples in the world would not help him if his carcass lay rotting out there in the desert.

For hours he rode, pacing himself and his horse. Shadow was holding up well, considering the workout his master had given him. He gamely trudged on, slowing only for an occasional blow or a drink of water.

Remington searched for the perfect spot but could not find it. He had laid it out in his mind, how it would be, how he would do it. At this point he was so tired that he did not think of adapting his plan to the available terrain. He did not want to allow for anything to go wrong.

The sun was an hour from setting when he found his spot.

He almost stumbled on it, detouring into this little gorge because a couple of fallen boulders had blocked his other path. He was almost past it before he realized it was just what he wanted.

Both sides of the hollow rose steeply away in gravelly slopes, just like the slippery ridge he had scrambled up in Hell's Door. A horse could not climb these, however. They were too steep.

The trail itself was narrow. The men would have to ride single file, or only two abreast at the widest part. And up above was a rocky shelf, ideal for a man to lie in wait.

He ranged back and forth until he found a trail to the top. Some spots were tricky going, but he coaxed the black upward until they reached some flatter ground near the ridge. He tied the gelding to a pinyon pine, then loaded his rifle.

Now it was just a matter of waiting.

The outlaws plodded along the tiny trail, just as he had known they would. Clagg was in the lead, so weary that his melon-sized head bobbed with every step his horse took. The others were strung out behind. Remington guessed they did not want to get too close, did not want to bump into each other, because their tempers were short.

Elongated shadows draped themselves across the rocks and depressions. A few more minutes and the sun would be going down.

Remington lay there, wedged between two boulders, his rifle already cocked. He did not want to make the mistake of letting even that minute noise echo off the cliffs and stone walls.

Isham Hyatt rode directly behind Clagg. Despite the distance, Remington could see the mad glaze in the killer's eyes. He would make as good a target as any.

The Henry roared through the ravine, knocking Hyatt from the saddle like a bolt of lightning.

Remington had planned it all out. He knew he had to hit several of them, and quickly. These were men of fast reflexes. It would not take them long to react.

His next target was at the other end of the string: Emmett Ballard. Ballard seemed to sense something, for he was just starting to yank his horse's head around when the bullet hit him.

He clutched at his chest. Remington did not have time to watch the damage. He sighted at Rudy Sumter and squeezed the trigger. All of those starved Yankee soldiers were avenged with a couple ounces of lead.

Clagg and some of the others were tossing back shots at him with their revolvers. The big Whitneyville Walker boomed like a peal of thunder, but even it was little more than an annoyance at that range.

One of the men, crazy with rage or gall or both, charged his horse straight up the slope, spurring the poor animal for all it was worth. Remington swung the Henry around and blasted him out of the saddle. As the outlaw skidded to the ground his horse stumbled back on the loose rocks and rolled over him in a kind of bizarre justice.

Clagg and his companions had dismounted. They leaned their long guns across their saddles, using their horses as shields.

Their fire became accurate, the slugs plucking and tearing at the rocks around the lawman.

Remington wanted to cut the odds by one more man before he made his escape. His choice was one of practicality. If they *did* catch him, he saw no need to compound his troubles by having Joe Ballard screaming for revenge for his slain brother.

The man raised his head for an instant, reloading. Remington put a slug just under the brim of his hat.

The marshal threw off several shots from the levergun, aiming them around the horses' hooves. The terrified animals began dancing, making just enough of a ruckus that the outlaws could not get a steady shot.

Remington leaped up from his hiding place, pebbles rolling and sliding under his boots. Keeping his head down, he made for the safety of the ridge.

Bullets scorched through the air around him, but as the light grew increasingly dim the dark-clothed figure was hard to pick out from the patchwork of shadows.

Before he had even set up the ambush, Remington had scouted out his escape path. It was a winding trail, almost parallel to the bottom of the gulch. He would have no trouble outdistancing the outlaws tonight.

The shooting stopped inside the draw. Not being sniped on anymore, the outlaws realized that Remington had escaped.

Apparently some of them chose the opportunity to make good their desertion. Remington could hear Ramsey Clagg's voice echoing up from the depths.

"Come back here, you yella bastards! Where the hell you think you're goin'? I said, come back here!"

Remington heard no replies. The darkness was falling quickly enough that the retreating men would be covered. Clagg could stew and fume, but even he knew better than to waste cartridges firing at the air.

The lawman figured Clagg and his buddies would camp soon to lick their wounds. One more ambush by the crafty marshal tonight might finish them. Best to ease off him until morning.

Remington did not try to rationalize what he had done. He

did try to push it out of his head so he could concentrate on the matters at hand.

After a mile or two, he noticed that something was odd about his horse. There was an unevenness to his gait. He would give a little shudder or shiver, but there were no flies to shake off.

Remington stopped and dismounted. That was when he saw it.

Below the animal's left hind leg was a small pool of blood.

Chapter Eleven

Remington made a furtive inspection of the horse's hide. It was too risky to light a match, so he just ran his fingers lightly over the coarse hair. After several seconds, he found it.

The marshal sighed with relief. It looked as though a bullet had not entered the flesh but had only grazed along it. There was a four-inch-long gash on the gelding's flank, oozing blood, but more slowly now. As Remington probed the sore the horse twitched, jumping to the side.

"Easy. Easy, Shadow. I know that's hurting you right now, but if you calm down, I'll try to make it better."

It was the tone of the man's voice more than his words that stopped the horse's fidgeting. This was the same man who always saw that he was fed and watered and, when they were in a town, made sure he got some grain and a combing out.

Remington dug in the saddlebag. He drew out some gauzy cloth and a small can of salve. It was an all-purpose ointment he had bought from a medicine show; it smelled terrible, but it had strong healing powers. Remington had used it on his own cuts and scratches, so he knew it worked.

He pried off the lid, gouging his finger into the gooey brown substance. He dabbed lightly at the edges of the cut, gradually working the salve toward it until the horse was used to the sensation. Remington knew that it had something of a numbing effect. He had no idea what was in it, but he was convinced of its potency.

Like a muddy poultice, the thick balm was stemming the flow of blood. That was what Remington wanted. Within minutes, the wound would start to dry over in a hard, crusty scab.

He made sure that the injury was well covered; then he stuck a small square of the bandage over it, to keep the flies away come sunup.

"I think we'd best walk you for a while, Shadow. We'll take some strain off and let you heal."

Taking the reins, the marshal led the gelding along the trail, pausing every so often to make certain blood was not seeping through the cloth.

Remington recognized that he was taking a chance, but he was too tired to press onward tonight. He was not as choosy about his campsite as he should have been. He needed to rest soon, though, and so did his horse.

The spot he picked was something of a rise on a larger hill, almost like a big bump. There were a few trees, some bushes, and even some mangy grass. All it lacked was water. Remington would find that in the morning.

Weary as he was, he still pitched the fake bedroll. He doubted that Clagg or any of the others would be searching for him again tonight, but, if anything in the past few days, he had learned that the redheaded man was unpredictable.

The horse looked dumbly at the lumpy bedroll for several seconds, then blinked at the man who was tossing out a blanket several yards away. He snorted once, then settled down into his own heavy sleep.

When Remington woke up for the first time, he pried out his pocket watch and saw that it was close enough to daylight to get up. He decided to give the gelding a couple more minutes. Taking some small tools and a bit of rag, Remington cleaned and oiled his weapons, examining them as best he could in the dim light.

The 1860 model Henry repeating rifle was a pretty gun, chambered for .44 caliber rimfire ammunition. Remington recalled a man who had told him that during the war a soldier could load it once in the morning and fire it all day. The marshal chugged the cartridges back into the tubular magazine. If it were not for this long gun, he would be virtually defenseless against the long-reaching Sharps of Ramsey Clagg.

He could not discount the worth of his Army model 1860 Colt's revolver. It was a conversion gun that had seen him through many a close fight. It slid into his palm as if the two had been made for each other.

After he tucked the pistol back into its holster, he stood up, stretched his legs, and flexed the kinks out of his back. He pulled up his blanket, shook the dust out of it, and started to roll it up.

Remington was surprised at the little grunt the horse gave him. Apparently it had already gotten its rest, because it was stretching its reins, munching on some of the coarse grass growing there. The tough marshal did not have the heart to interrupt the gelding's breakfast. The horse had earned it— and much better.

Walking around the camp for a few minutes to limber up, Remington became aware of how bone-weary tired he really was. It was not the same sluggishness that comes after a day of hard work; he felt a hundred years old and ached all over.

The few hours' rest would allow him to go on the rest of the day—the sleep and a big chunk of willpower—but he knew damn well he could not keep this up forever.

He wondered how Clagg was holding out. Remington had one thing over on the buffalo hunter. The lawman did not have that tremendous bulk to support. Remington laughed when he thought of the scene after the ambush. He could almost imagine Clagg searching the saddlebags of the dead men's horses, looking not for valuables but for food. He had likely not anticipated such a long hunt. Remington had been prepared from the start.

The other men would be grumbling and grousing as well. Did outlaws share with one another? Would Clagg offer his hungry companions some of his food?

Thinking of eating brought the rumbling back to Remington's gut. Walking down, he saw two serviceberry bushes, thick with fruit that was just starting to ripen. These plants, farther south, must have been ahead in the growing season.

He helped himself to several handfuls of the berries,

flinching at first at their tartness, then relishing the welcome change in his diet. He let them linger on his tongue, chewing up the tough skins. They would hold him until he partook of the monotonous crackers and jerky around noon. But at least he had that. Maybe Clagg and the others had run out of grub by now. That would help him too. One more hardship might make these men decide to turn back.

Of course, they could shoot a jackrabbit or a prairie chicken during the day, if they wanted to take the time to stop and cook it. Remington wondered if they would eat it raw. They might, if they were hungry enough.

Ned Remington was a man with no family, few possessions. He did not give much thought to such things, but he did enjoy a good meal. Living as he did, from day to day, he took satisfaction in simple pleasures.

Once again he pictured the rusty-haired waitress in that Amarillo café. He would like to take her to the nicest restaurant in town, just to see those green eyes across the table from him and to hear her laugh. There were few things that pleased him more than a woman's clear, honest laugh.

"Well, big fella, if you've stuffed yourself enough, it's time for me to mount up. What do you say?"

The horse shook its head, but there were no flies to be brushing off. Remington grinned.

"I'm sick of running too, Shadow, but maybe it won't be for much longer," he said quietly.

He got his tack together and lashed it securely to the saddle with rawhide thongs. The Henry was safe in its boot and the Colt was safely back in his holster. Remington swung up, pulling his hat down.

Twisting behind him, he checked the condition of the wound on the horse's flank. The blood had coagulated into a hard brown scab. The little patch of cloth was thoroughly stuck inside it, which would keep flies and bugs from burrowing into the wound. Remington thought that just the smell of the salve would keep any vermin away. Hard riding might be pushing it, but the marshal was reasonably sure the wound would not break open again.

They cut down the side of the hill in the predawn haze.

Remington did not like the prospects for the rest of the day. The country was starting to favor the outlaws. It was turning flat, with fewer obstructions between him and their rifles.

The sun had just broken orange over the horizon ahead of him. Remington started the gelding out slow, trying to limber him up first before he put much pressure on the wound. If it broke open and the horse began to lose blood again, he could weaken fast. In this heat, loss of blood could bring on a rapid collapse.

The black shook his head, danced, frisky after a good night's rest. Remington had to rein him back. He wished that he was experiencing that same kind of energy.

As the light got better Remington looked back at the scab once more. It was healing nicely. He had had the horse well hidden.

Remington kept glancing over his shoulder. After a half hour, he saw them. They were only a couple of black specks, but they were there, still pursuing him. He chanced a look at them through the telescope, staying in the saddle so as not to lose any time.

The marshal was astonished to see only three men.

He had not expected his ambush to have such a devastating effect. Just two others accompanied Clagg. The rest—he estimated there had been four or five survivors of his attack besides these three—must have been too injured or too disgusted to go on. They were still too far away for him to make out their faces, and he had no intention of letting them get closer.

A noise reverberated to him, like a clattering of shod hooves on stony ground; then, when he saw the dust being chucked up some twenty or thirty feet away, he realized they were shooting at him.

Remington peered through the glass again to see Clagg turned toward the other men. The outlaw did not have his rifle out. His companions put theirs away.

As he stowed the glass Remington figured out what was happening. These two men had probably had it with taking orders. They were ready to stop him any way they could, either by wounding his horse or by knocking him out of the saddle. Clagg, mean and intimidating though he was, could keep only a loose rein over them.

That told Remington he had to be even more careful. The outlaws had been pushed past the breaking point. They must have figured Clagg should be grateful to have them along, so they were pressing his patience as much as they could.

Remington wondered why Clagg thought he even needed them. Surely he was not afraid to track the lawman alone. But these men might come in handy in laying a trap. They were expendable, and if they could bring the marshal out in the open . . .

He vowed not to let such a situation happen. He would be watching for it. If, at any time, the three men split up, he would know Clagg was hiding somewhere with a cocked rifle.

Something else made the lawman's eyes narrow. Each of the three outlaws was trailing a spare horse behind him, undoubtedly the mounts of the dead men.

Remington knew what that meant. They could ride their first horses until they dropped—and Clagg probably would— then they could switch to the other mounts. Clagg knew that the marshal's black could outrun any of their horses, but it did not have the endurance of *two* animals.

The wound on Shadow's flank compounded matters. Remington would have to nurse the gelding along, at least through most of the morning, hoping that the sore would bind as the day wore on. If Clagg and his pals chose to make a run toward him soon, they could end it.

Remington snapped himself back to reality. They did not know about the gelding's injury, unless they had seen the blood. Even then, they might have thought it came from Remington. Anticipating trouble could help him be prepared, but there was no sense worrying about something that might not happen.

He kept a tight rein on the gelding, satisfied with their steady progress. As far as Remington could tell, the three men were not gaining on him. If he could maintain that gap, he would buy time until he thought of something.

Remington understood that it would not go on this way for long. Clagg would pick his moment well. They would follow for several hours, keeping up the pressure, pushing their horses, making Remington run; then they would change to the fresh mounts and overtake him. The plan was pretty obvious.

A perfectly good solution came into Remington's head. He smiled when he thought of it. Clagg would not expect it; neither would the others.

The gelding kept up a good pace for the remainder of the morning. As they continued east the ground got more level, with gently rolling hills starting to blend down toward the plain. Clagg would pick a flat, even stretch for his attack.

Remington put himself inside the big man's head. Chasing such an elusive foe, he would probably work the same type of scheme he was sure Clagg was planning. It would force him to spend his horse; then he could simply be run down. It was simple, but it could work.

The sun was at its zenith. Sweat was rolling off Remington, dribbling down his forehead, collecting between his shoulder blades and sliding down his back.

He thought the horse could not take much more. Maybe he would have to stop soon, cool him. If he could find a place with some cover, where Shadow would be out of the way of the outlaws' bullets, he could hold them off while the horse got a rest.

The gap between them started to close.

Clagg was still biding his time, riding steadily. Their horses had to be pushed hard too. Maybe they were ready to trade them off.

Remington scouted the land ahead. Nothing stood out as a defensive position. Here and there were some clumps of locust and gambel oak, but they would afford poor protection.

The gelding slowed, stumbling once, breaking his rolling rhythm. He needed rest, and he needed it soon.

If Remington stopped in the open, or even behind one of the small groups of trees, the outlaws would keep their distance, tossing shots at his mount.

Clagg and the two others slowed down, brought their

horses to a stop. They dismounted. Remington watched them, through his telescope, tightening the cinches and changing their guns and gear to the fresh animals.

They were starting to run.

For a long time he just let the gelding walk along as the trio gained on him. He gave an occasional look over his shoulder, saw they were getting closer.

The marshal knew the range of his Henry rifle, within a few yards.

Remington put himself inside Clagg's mind once more. The big man was charging hard. The lawman was hardly moving. He was not trying to get away. Maybe the gelding was too tired for that. It made no difference. In a minute or two, they would overtake the bastard of a marshal.

The waiting was hard. It was like playing poker, hesitating until the last second, not letting the other fellow guess your play.

With the fluidity of an Indian, Remington swung down from his horse, in the same motion sliding the Colt out of its holster.

He sat on the ground. He balanced his left arm on his knee. The first shot found its mark.

The outlaw to Clagg's right pitched backward, clutching his chest. He fell out of the saddle and hit the ground with such force that if the bullet had not killed him, the spill probably broke his neck.

Clagg and the other man jerked back on the reins so hard they pulled their horses' heads sideways.

In that split second, they knew the next lead would be for them. Remington triggered a shot toward the man to Clagg's left, but the outlaw's horse was prancing so much that the bullet went wide.

The two bandits did not have time to pull their rifles out. The marshal was throwing shots at them. Continuing the charge would be suicide, riding right into his gunsights.

Remington pitched more shots in front of their horses. He wanted to scare the animals, and he did. They backstepped on their own. Even if Clagg and the other man tried to get their rifles out, they would be worthless atop such nervous horses.

For a second, Remington held his breath.

Clagg might try to dismount, sit or lie on the ground, and do the same thing. He might even shoot his dead companion's horse and use it for cover.

But the thought apparently never came to him. Remington could understand why, with lead flying all about and nothing to hide behind.

The two men fell back, retreating behind a stand of trees.

Remington mounted again as soon as they were hidden. They had ridden out of his range, and he knew it. But that was what he had wanted all along. That, and reducing the odds against him some more.

He tried to imagine the conversation—or shouting match —Clagg and his buddy were having. Each of them probably had a brilliant plan for catching up with the lawman. The problem was that their *last* brilliant plan had not worked.

The gelding had caught its second wind. Remington took it easier this time, going as slowly as he could with the big black, yet still staying out of Clagg's rifle range.

And Clagg made sure to keep his distance from the sharpshooting lawman. They made no more tries at a run that afternoon.

Remington's horse cooled down some, but he needed rest, food, and water. The scabby sore was still holding up. They had not galloped enough to cause it to crack.

Remembering his impression of Clagg from their card game at Hell's Door, and from the kinds of crimes he had committed, Remington knew that the buffalo hunter felt no great sadness at the loss of his latest companion. The dead man was probably considered just another casualty of this hell-bent-for-leather chase, an unfortunate incident that would make it that much harder for Clagg.

Remington could almost sense the hatred seething inside the big man. What he had done to Pete Trask would look merciful compared to what he would do to this marshal if he ever got his hands on him.

By midafternoon, Remington got an idea. He pulled the sweat-stained map out of his shirt and shook it open. Trask's pencil scrawlings were becoming blurred, but it was evident the land only got flatter to the east.

So Remington took a wide swing north and began gradually heading west again.

It was a big risk. Clagg could not cut him off and try to intercept him, but it meant more rambling through the rugged ground, prolonging the chase and increasing the distance.

About sunset, Remington came to a shallow river. He consulted the map, but the stream was not shown there. It was probably too small, or maybe Trask had not traveled this part of the country. The water was brown and flowing fast. It did not reach even to the gelding's knees.

Remington dismounted. He splashed water on his head, soaked his hat, then wrung it out. It took the heat out of him immediately.

He walked the horse down the center of the stream for nearly a mile. That would delay Clagg and his partner a bit. It would give Remington a breather.

The marshal estimated that by the time his two pursuers got to the river, it would be dark. They would see his tracks leading in. When they did not come out directly on the other side, Clagg would be able to figure what had happened. Maybe he would wait until morning before trying to pick them up again.

Remington was counting on that. It was mighty enticing, a campsite by a river. He would be camped upstream, a mile and a half, but they would not know that.

Weariness is a powerful temptress. Few men can resist it. Even Ned Remington had to succumb tonight. He could try another raid on Clagg's camp. One of them would be standing watch, sure. If it was the other outlaw, Remington could take him from a distance with his throwing knife, then get the drop on Clagg.

But he was just too damn bone-tired. His reflexes were like cold molasses, and he knew it. A fraction of an inch and he could miss a crucial knife toss. *That* would mean the end of him, an excruciatingly slow and agonizing end.

So the marshal pitched camp, hoping for a shaky truce of sorts, like the truce between men who had battered each other and themselves into exhaustion in a fistfight, each too weak to throw even one more punch.

Remington found some more wild berries along the stream. His horse located enough green, lush grass to make him swish his tail in contentment as he grazed on it.

Darkness settled down like a thick black shawl. Remington sat on a little rise, enjoying the cool evening breeze, pushing cartridges into the Henry. The box he had bought back in— where was it? Sable—it was gertting very low.

Then he saw it.

It required an instant decision.

He brought back what he knew about Ramsey Clagg, all of the information mentioned on the wanted posters, what Judge Barnstall had told him, what Tully and Virgil had said, what he himself had observed in the outlaw camp.

Little more than a second had passed when Ned raised the Henry. He knew as he sighted in that it was a stupid action.

Yet one of those bizarre hunches, the kind that had kept him alive in the past, told him to do it. He knew it was hopeless as soon as he felt the steel trigger warming to the touch of his finger.

It was the tiniest of things that he saw, yet on a night as black as this one, it stood out at even that great distance. They were camped closer to him than he had thought.

He pointed the gun at it. It was the most minute of flickerings, the momentary burning of a match that would soon be out.

But Remington knew that Ramsey Clagg did not smoke. And he would not be stupid enough to build a fire. It meant only one thing.

Clagg's partner, confident he was safe, was lighting a cigarette.

Remington's shot had not stopped echoing when he heard the scream. Then it died away, just as the man did who made it.

A simple, stupid act of lighting a cigarette. Even Remington admitted to himself that the shot had been a fluke, a bit of fortune he would never be able to duplicate. He did not know the distance. It had to be at least a couple hundred yards.

Now the odds were even.

It was just him and Clagg.

Chapter Twelve

Remington thought that the smartest thing he could do would be to break camp and find another position, one far away from Ramsey Clagg and his now-dead companion.

The marshal had not realized that the outlaws were settled so close to him, but it felt *too* close after he eliminated Clagg's final pawn. Remington was tired. He was weary, stretched almost to the point of exhaustion, and he did not want to spend another night sleeping with one eye open, expecting the big buffalo hunter to come creeping up on him in the dark.

Since Remington's camps were never elaborate, it did not take him long to relocate. The thing that took him the most time was folding up the phony bedroll. He wondered if it would fool a man as cunning as Clagg. After coming this far, Remington was not about to underestimate him.

The marshal was tempted—but only for a moment—to close in on Clagg and try to end this thing, here, now. But he took stock of the situation. It was not in his favor. He was a realist. He knew how tired he was. He recognized that his reflexes were slow. That fraction of a second, that difference that most men would never even notice, could well cost him his life with someone like Ramsey Clagg.

So he would bide his time. He was not happy about it, but he understood how necessary it was. Maybe tomorrow he would be more rested. Maybe tomorrow he would find a spot that would lend itself to what he wanted to do. Maybe tomorrow some quirk of fate would put Ramsey Clagg at the disadvantage.

For the past couple of days, luck had been in Remington's favor. He was not a great believer in luck, never counted on it to pull him through, never put his fate up to chance when he could manipulate it by his own hand, but he was shrewd enough to admit that luck existed.

That shot, that incredible, impossible, once-in-a-lifetime shot in the dark that evened the odds with the outlaw, might have been Remington's last bit of luck. He took his time finding a new camp, convinced that it would be nearly dawn by the time Clagg could find it. By then Remington would be gone.

The lawman had something of a built-in alarm clock. He did not know how it worked. He simply told himself that he wanted to get so many hours' sleep, and he usually woke within a few minutes of when he wanted to. It was a talent that he had had since boyhood.

This day he wanted to wake long enough before dawn to backtrack to the outlaw's camp, to be waiting for him when the sun started over the winding, twisting trail he had left. By the first rays, he was in position.

As the light evaporated the mysteries of the landscape, Remington put his spyglass to his eye and scanned the spot where the man had lit the fateful cigarette only a handful of hours ago. The body was still there, flat on its back, the hand-rolled quirley grotesquely clutched between stiffened fingers.

Ramsey Clagg was nowhere to be seen.

Remington roamed the telescope left and right, looking for thin shadows on hoof-printed soil. Both horses were gone. A few scraggly trees hugged the banks of the stream, but they were hardly enough cover for the big man and two mounts.

It was a situation Remington should have expected. Letting the killer catch him off guard showed the marshal just how tired he really was. He should have been able to predict this move. It was not so different from what *he* would have done.

The first shot tore through the brim of Remington's hat, barely three inches from the crown.

He rolled for cover, snatching the hanging reins of his horse even as he found a hole. Remington commanded the

horse to lie down. The gelding settled in next to him, its eyes
wide at the sound of gunfire.

They were in a ditch five or six feet deep and a dozen feet
across. Bullets whizzed over the top of it. Remington wished
he could make the horse duck its head, but that was a trick the
animal had never mastered.

The lawman had thought he was on the highest ground in
the area, but he had been wrong. Clagg was out there somewhere, sniping down on him. The big man had guessed exactly where his foe would light, to get his first look at the
camp. All Clagg had needed was first sunlight to show him
his target.

Remington wondered whether the outlaw had missed him
on purpose.

Now it was a question of whether Clagg wanted to murder
him outright or wanted to make a game of it. If he *could* get
the drop on Remington there would be no one around to watch
Clagg indulge his sport. Did he need an audience? He hadn't
had one when he had so brutally put an end to Pete Trask.

Remington had memorized this piece of land earlier. Even
crouching down in this gully, he could see what the buzzards
soaring overhead saw. He laid it out in his mind's eye, placing
Clagg on a rise off to the east. He recalled a grove of trees, a
sharp bend in the river, a hill of sorts with a stretch of weeds
and grass on it.

The lawman wondered if the grass would be dry enough to
catch fire. It could give him the chance he needed.

Remington stuck his head up, then jerked it back down.
The grass was over there to his left, about twenty or thirty feet
out. The wind was blowing in the right direction, just a light,
early-morning breeze.

Searching around the ditch, Remington found just the size
clod of dirt he wanted. He wrapped some of the gauzy bandage from his saddlebag around it. Positioning himself closer
to his horse, he struck a match, lit the trailing scrap of fabric,
then cocked his arm and heaved the burning projectile toward
the patch of weeds.

Within a few seconds, a crackling, sizzling noise came

back to him. Then he saw the first signs of the brown-gray smoke. The grass was just dry enough.

At first the wind shifted, pushing tufts of smoke over the trench. Shadow nearly bolted at the smell of fire, but Remington hung on tightly to the reins.

Then the breeze returned to its original direction, fueling the flames and sending the clouds in Clagg's vicinity. Remington waited.

He knew the smoke would not be thick enough to cover him. He was not counting on that. What he wanted was a steady stream of eye-stinging fumes, enough of an irritant that the outlaw would not be able to get a clear shot at him.

Remington chanced another look. No shot came at him this time. He saw that the licking fire was quickly consuming the little patch. Now was the time.

He urged the horse to its feet and mounted. The gelding needed little prompting. Bounding up the side of the ravine, he kicked out across the plain, away from the fire and the confounded Ramsey Clagg.

Remington had let Clagg get the upper hand on him, whether from fatigue or overconfidence, it did not matter. The marshal would not rationalize away his error. It could very well have cost him his life. He suspected that the buffalo hunter had missed him on purpose with that first shot.

The grass had been there, the wind had been blowing the right way, he had managed to get the fire to it and it took. Remington had gotten out of this one, but he knew it might not happen so easily next time. He did not want to feel Ramsey Clagg's skinning knife slicing into his flesh as Pete Trask had.

Last night, just after he had killed the outlaw with the cigarette, the marshal had expected Clagg to come after him. Clagg knew by now that the lawman did not intend to kill him. He was so sure that Remington had vowed to take him back alive that he had become cocky.

A thin smile grew on Remington's face. If this situation were not so deadly, it would be funny. Both men knew the other was not going to kill him outright. Both were trying to trick the other into making that fatal mistake.

Clagg had two horses now, Remington reminded himself. He had taken the dead man's mount and likely he would use it to his advantage. Maybe *now* he would try putting the run on the marshal, for he knew Remington would not blast him out of the saddle.

Remington kept riding, pushing, opening up as much ground as he could between himself and the red-bearded outlaw. He was sure Clagg would continue to follow him; he had lost too much to give up now. And the blood hate would carry him through until this thing was done with, one way or another.

Ramsey Clagg was a driven man, just as much as Ned Remington was. The lawman reasoned that the difference between them, though, was that *he* was only doing his job, a job he had done hundreds of times before, and even though this man was tougher than most, he was still just a criminal who had to be brought in. Clagg, on the other hand, was being pushed by whatever lust inhabits a killer's crazed mind. He had the cunning of a mountain lion, but somewhere along the way he had let his emotions enter the picture.

The marshal wondered whether Clagg had crossed the point where cold, rational thinking guided him and had become consumed by a lust for revenge.

Unpredictability was how Clagg had almost caught him; now he would turn the tables. Remington thought it was time for him to go on the offensive.

What would the outlaw do if suddenly the marshal turned and started hunting *him?*

The first thing Remington wanted to do was separate Clagg from that spare horse. If he could not do it by trick, he would be forced to kill the animal. Remington saw that as a last resort, but the mount was certainly expendable in the name of justice. On the great scales, it could not balance out the need to avenge the deaths of Pete Trask and Sarah O'Keefe.

For three hours the marshal rode until he found exactly the spot he wanted. Since he had doubled back and turned northwest, the terrain had become more rugged again.

The place he picked was not obvious. He doubted even Clagg would expect it. The plan hinged on split-second timing. If the outlaw followed Remington's tracks, he would come through a narrow draw, but he would only be there for a moment. Remington would have one shot, two at most, and he would have to make them count.

This time Remington made sure the big gelding was well hidden. He wanted no stray bullets doing any more damage to the black.

Remington took up a position in a thicket of low juniper, his rifle barrel down and coated with a film of light dust to prevent any glare. He estimated Clagg was somewhere between a half hour and an hour behind him.

The minutes went by like a stampede of snails. Remington lay motionless in the brush, listening intently for the sound of the big man's horses on the trail. All he heard was a rasping wind and the occasional flitting of a bird from tree to tree.

The juniper smelled clean, fresh. The aroma masked Remington's own perspiration. Every so often a fly would land on the back of his neck and bite it, sitting there casually sucking his blood. He blinked his eyes but resisted the urge to swat. He was not about to lose his life over a damn insect.

Remington was a good judge of time. He figured an hour had dragged by before he dared to move. It was only the slightest twisting of his head so he could see the land around him. For all he knew, Clagg might be perched somewhere, just waiting to draw a bead on him.

Remington waited another fifteen minutes before he slid and scooted out of his hiding place. He held his breath. No shots came. Pulling his hat down to shade his eyes from the pounding sun, he gazed across the tangle of small hills and valleys.

No motion of man came to his ears. No birds skittered away from the sound of an approaching intruder. Remington even sniffed the air, thinking he might catch the scent of the unwashed buff'ler. There was no clue that the man was anywhere within miles.

The marshal smiled as he gently let the hammer down on the Henry. Clagg was as contrary as a band of Apaches. The big man knew the marshal wanted him. He knew that Remington had come all the way out here for the sole purpose of hauling him back to Missouri.

Now he was going to make the lawman come to him.

Remington saw the raw genius in the plan. He did want Clagg. He did intend to keep up this damnable game until it ended in a showdown.

Fetching his horse, Remington acknowledged that he had no other choice. He had to go after Clagg now.

And as sure as he rode for the law, Remington knew that Clagg was setting a trap for him.

Most of the afternoon Remington rode, following his own tracks backward. He tried to conserve his horse's energy, resting it when he could, letting it drink or graze when he dared. Clagg was running, but he would not run away. It was obvious that he wanted their paths to cross.

Remington expected to be back at the river before he caught the outlaw's trail, but that would have been too predictable. The marshal picked up hoofprints from a pair of horses on a sandy ridge.

He drove hard, trying to catch up. After a half hour he learned that Clagg had wanted to outdistance him. The big man had changed horses.

The horse he left behind, a sorrel mare, was all but spent. It eyed Remington wildly when he approached it. Lather flecked its coat, and its left front leg was weak.

Remington moved on. Ramsey Clagg had a fairly fresh horse, but he was down to one now. The odds were more even, expect that Clagg might be setting an ambush up ahead, just as Remington had done. The marshal could turn and hope to get Clagg to follow *him* again, but he was sick of this game of cat and mouse. It was time to take a chance, time to bring it to a close.

Darkness was closing down when the shots whined around Remington.

He wheeled his horse, backing it fifteen feet, then followed a cutoff on a narrow side trail. The shots had come close together, and, judging from the sound of them, Remington knew they had come from Clagg's Walker pistol. Was the outlaw that close that he thought he could hit something with a sidearm?

More shots came. Even in the blackness, Remington knew they were nowhere close to him. He could hear the scream of an occasional ricochet, but the bullets did not fly around him as they had a few moments ago.

He dismounted and sought cover behind a boulder. Some scrubby trees served to break up his horse's silhouette.

"That was just a little warnin', lawman!" Clagg's raspy voice boomed out over the hills. "I'm gonna get you. Make no mistake about that. What I done to Trask'll look like play compared to what I got in mind for you."

Remington tried to place the voice. The echoes and the enveloping darkness made it impossible. The big man was farther away than he had first thought, possibly mounted. Probably he had fired both volleys from horseback. That meant he would make a fast retreat.

There were no more shots. Apparently the taunting was over, Remington thought. That was all Clagg had intended to do—unnerve him.

After scouting about for a few minutes, Remington learned that he was in a fairly safe spot to make camp for the night. Clagg was unpredictable; he might come back, but the lawman was counting that Clagg would keep up the flight to try to lure him into a trap after daybreak.

Remington could see what was coming. Clagg would lie in wait, try to shoot the marshal's horse from under him, then worry him with long-range shots. If Remington tried to get away on foot, Clagg would run him down. If he tried to make a stand of it, the big man would wait him out or attempt to take him at night.

It did not leave him much of a choice. Remington knew he would be riding into a trap. It was only a question now of where and when. That was all part of Clagg's strategy too, to try to rattle the lawman so he would make a costly mistake.

He would need all of his wits about him in the morning. That was when it would come to an end.

Remington tied his horse securely and turned in. He did

not bother with the fake bedroll this night. Clagg was probably too smart to fall for it, anyway.

Clagg was not going to chance a hand-to-hand fight tonight. Something might go wrong, Remington might get killed, and that would spoil all his fun. It would happen tomorrow.

Tomorrow.

When he crawled out of his bedroll a half hour before dawn, Remington sensed that something was wrong. It was nothing definite, just a gnawing hunch that something was badly amiss.

He moved slowly at first. It was possible that Clagg might be camped off somewhere, ready to blast down on him at the sun's first rays. He did not want to make any noise, risk giving away his position.

Remington rolled up his blankets and gear and made it over to his horse. It was then that he discovered it.

The big gelding had come up lame.

He walked the black around for a bit, watching it favor its left front leg. This put a different turn on things. It cut off Remington's chance for a quick escape, if need be. It meant that he could not track Clagg if the outlaw chose to run.

Remington was not totally surprised. He had been pushing the horse way too hard for the last week anyway. The gelding was an extraordinary animal, but he was not supernatural. It was inevitable that something had to give.

The damage appeared to be only a pulled muscle or a twisted ankle. The injury would heal in time, but right now time was something Remington did not have.

His mind raced, trying to come up with solutions to this problem. Every time, the scene came out the same—him suspended upside down from a tree like Trask had been, with Clagg carving on his naked body with a red-hot knife.

Remington led the horse back the way they had come, not exactly sure where they were going. He did know that there was nothing along that trail that would save him. He had passed no towns or farms or houses.

He decided to cut away and head directly north. He probably would not get far on foot before Clagg came looking for him. Well, he would react to that situation when it presented itself.

Remington consulted Pete Trask's map again. Where the pencil scrawls were too jammed together to fit in anything else, Trask had scribbled in tiny numbers, keyed to explanations written on the reverse side.

Something caught the marshal's eye, a minute notation he might have missed had he not been searching so desperately for a plan. There was a very small number 8 written in, so light and smudged that it was almost invisible. Remington checked the opposite side of the paper. Near the number 8 was a note about a black rock cliff fronting a dry wash.

Remington had just passed that!

It would have been of no consequence except that a few miles to the north was the farm of Elson O'Keefe, and Remington was sure that the man had a fresh horse he would let him use.

Once he had his bearings, Remington started to move north, as fast as he dared with the injured horse. He contemplated leaving the animal behind and running to O'Keefe's farm, but he was not sure just how far it was. If Clagg, on horseback, caught up to him, he would have no chance to escape.

So far there had been no sign of his pursuer. Remington hoped that Clagg was miles away, laying his ambush on some deserted trail. That would give the marshal time to get to the farmer, get a new horse, then backtrack toward the outlaw. Maybe he would even be able to pick up Clagg's track, cut a wide loop, and get the drop on *him*.

The country was hilly, just at the edge of what would become mountains. O'Keefe's farm was set in a valley between two high ridges. It might be over the next rise, or there might be a dozen ridges between Remington and the farm. He was not sure. This kind of terrain was deceptive, and Remington couldn't waste time riding in circles.

A twig snapping behind him sounded as loud as a gunshot.

Remington spun, whipping out his six-gun even as he moved.

"No shoot. You no shoot. Joseph Two-Shoes friend."

It was an old Navajo, his wrinkled face shaded by a battered black hat. Remington was not as interested in the Indian as he was in the pretty little paint pony he was sitting on.

"Joseph Two-Shoes? That your name?"

"Yes. That is what I am called. I am friend. Do not shoot."

"I'm not going to shoot you," Remington said, holstering his gun. "What are you doing wandering around in these hills?"

A trace of a smile crossed the old man's lips. "I have been in these hills since I was a boy. I work not far from here. Have job."

"My name's Remington. I'm a United States chief territorial marshal from far to the east. I'm looking for a man, a very bad man, a robber and a killer named Ramsey Clagg. He's a big fella, much bigger than me, with hair and beard the color of fire. Have you seen him in these hills?"

The old man's face grew even longer. "No. Have seen no one except you."

"That horse of yours," Remington said. "Consider trading him?"

"For your lame horse?" The Indian chuckled. "Why I do that?"

"You've got a point. Well, take a look at my horse. The damage to his leg isn't bad. Besides, I just want your horse for a . . . loan. I don't want to get rid of my horse."

"You want to trade, but you do not want to trade?" Joseph Two-Shoes was confused.

"How about this? You let me borrow your horse for a day or two, you take my horse, and I'll give you"—he dug in his pocket—"ten dollars in gold."

"I get my horse back?"

"Yes. It's just a loan."

"First gold." He held his palm out. Remington put the coin in it.

"He's saddle-broke?" Remington asked as the Navajo dismounted.

"He used to my saddle."

The saddle the Indian pointed to was little more than a few scraps of leather and some stirrups, with a wool blanket padding. It was nothing like the high-cantled, big-horned cowboy's saddle on Remington's gelding. But at this point he could not argue.

"I'll take my rifle and my saddlebags," Remington said. "How will I find you when I come back?"

"Go to farm. I work at farm. I leave horse there. No good to ride till leg get better."

"Okay, Joseph Two-Shoes. I'll be back for him in a day or two. You take good care of him, hear?"

"What if you . . . not *come* back?"

"Then the horse and saddle are yours."

Remington jumped up on the paint. It was a small, nervous animal, not more than a few years old, but it felt strong under him. He knew it could not have the wind of the gelding, yet he sensed it could deliver terrific speed in short bursts.

"This horse have a name?" Remington inquired.

"I just call him Horse."

"Makes sense. The black's name is Shadow." The paint responded to his reins and his knees and wheeled about. It would take them a while to get used to each other.

Remington backtracked for the better part of an hour, hoping to intersect Clagg's trail. He was coming up blank.

These hills were a maze. That was why he had returned to them, but now they were working against him. The outlaw had the advantage and he was making good use of it.

Remington swiveled, scanning the landscape in all directions. When he looked behind him, in the area where he had traded for the fresh horse, he saw it. A sickening knot seized his empty stomach.

A thick, rolling cloud of smoke was billowing up in the distance.

Chapter Thirteen

Remington did not have to consult the map again. He knew where the smoke was coming from. It had to be the farm of Elson O'Keefe.

The marshal urged the little pinto on with his bootheels, but he found that it needed scant prodding. The horse was a natural runner and had enough high-strung energy to carry him for miles.

Going was rough. There really were no wide, flat, open expanses where he could give the pony his head. Still, he took the twisting trails and steep ravines as agilely as if he were cutting calves on the plain.

Remington could not get there soon enough. The thought that it might be a trap occurred to him. It would be just like Clagg to use an innocent person to lure him in. He could not let that stop him.

He wondered about Elson O'Keefe. Had the farmer seen the big man coming? Had he opened up on him with the old Spencer?

Maybe it had gone the other way. Clagg was a crafty one. He had hit this farm before. He might suspect that the man would be more wary now. The outlaw had no way of knowing that his rape had killed the woman. He had no way of understanding the thoughts that raced through Elson O'Keefe's mind in lonely moments. It would not be like him, though, on the run, to just waltz in and not expect some kind of welcoming committee.

Remington wished he could see over the ridges and through the trees. The smoke was still rolling upward in great black balls. When Remington topped the hill, the sight from down in the valley made him want to retch. The flames were wrapped around O'Keefe's wooden house, eating at it like orange demons.

The lawman raced his horse down the slope. Twice the pony nearly stumbled; then it started to run so fast Remington wondered whether it would be able to stop. He eased back on the reins, and it got the message. Its beating hooves slowed. By the time they approached the farmyard, the paint was moving at a slow trot.

Remington had seen nothing of Clagg from the rise. That did not mean he was not there. He could be in the barn, his big Sharps drawing aim even now. He could be lying in some bushes on the other hillside.

After all, Remington had not seen his corpse either.

Where was Elson O'Keefe?

Remington dismounted, tying the pony a safe distance from the fire. Sparks were drifting in the updraft, blowing this way and that. The green leaves of an overhanging tree had been singed to blackness.

The marshal ran into the barn. "O'Keefe? Elson O'Keefe! You in here?"

No answer.

The horses were there, stamping nervously between the barn and the corral, so that meant O'Keefe had not gone on a trip. Even if he were in a far corner of the field, he would be able to see the plume of smoke.

Glancing at the house from the open barn door, Remington noticed a charred, broken lantern on the front porch. Flames had already scorched the doorway black and were enveloping the porch roof.

There was no other choice. Remington had to go inside that burning house.

He dashed back inside the barn and ripped a thick wool blanket off the cot. Running to the edge of the corral, he dunked the blanket in the horse trough, making sure it was thoroughly soaked. He pulled his hat down on his head, flung the blanket over his shoulders, and ran toward the flaming cabin.

The heat pushed against him like a giant hand. He could almost feel the blanket drying out with each step he took.

One kick turned the door to splinters. It was already burned through.

Remington stumbled into the front room. The air was too stifling even to expend the effort on cursing. He kept the blanket drawn up around his face, but flames seemed to be gouging at his eyes.

O'Keefe was not in that room. The smoke was stinging, hanging in the place like a thick gray fog. Remington began to cough, unable to control himself.

The house had only two rooms. Remington pushed back toward the rear. The bedroom door was open. When his own coughing subsided for a second, he heard another rasping voice.

At first he thought it was the gravelly throat of Ramsey Clagg. He wanted to draw his pistol, but he did not want to lose the protection of the blanket.

Backing to the side of the opening, he took a chance.

"O'Keefe? That you?"

"Remington?" More coughing. "Remington?"

Remington stepped across into the room. O'Keefe was at a chest of drawers, gathering some cheap glass knickknacks into a burlap bag. He also had a wet blanket wrapped around him, but the bottom edges of his cover were smoldering.

"What the hell are you doing, man? Let's get out of here. This place is going to come down any second," Remington said.

"In a minute."

He grabbed O'Keefe's arm. "There isn't *time*. Let's go!"

"No, dammit!" The farmer shook loose. "Don't you understand. These are all I've got left of her. She bought them on our honeymoon."

There was a wild look in the man's eyes, the most incredible, frenzied, pained expression the lawman had ever seen on another human being's face.

"Okay," Remington relented, swearing under his breath at his own insanity. He walked over and helped O'Keefe pack the trinkets.

Once the dresser top was clean, the marshal pushed O'Keefe ahead of him toward the door. But a timber had fallen down from the ceiling, blocking their escape.

"Out the window," Remington ordered.

O'Keefe picked up a straight-backed wooden chair and poked its legs through the panes of glass. Knocking the remaining shards away with a blanket-wrapped hand, he motioned to Remington. "You go first."

"Get the hell out of here!" He had to restrain himself from putting his boot to the farmer.

O'Keefe crawled through, Remington close at his heels. Hot pitch, each droplet bearing a tiny flame, dripped from the room, scorching small holes in their blankets.

The two men trotted away from the building, O'Keefe holding his treasure close to him.

Once they were in the clear, Remington shouted at him. "You could've got yourself killed in there, Elson. And for what? A bunch of colored pieces of glass?"

"I wouldn't expect you to understand, Marshal," the man returned, peering down into the sack to see if anything had been broken. "You never had a woman like my Sarah."

The marshal looked at the man's reddened, smudged face, his home being destroyed behind him, then slowly said, "You're right, Elson. You're right. I guess I never did."

"It's gone," O'Keefe said, shaking his head. "It's gone."

"Those sparks are drifting toward the barn and the henhouse," Remington said. "C'mon! Let's get buckets. There's still time to save them."

They ran to the barn and got all the buckets, pails, and large cans they could find. O'Keefe manned the pump while Remington sped back and forth, wetting down the roofs.

A half hour later, the fire from the house had died down and the sparks were no longer dancing on the wind. All that remained of the wooden cabin was a smoking black skeleton and a naked rock chimney.

"Well, we managed to save the barn, at least," O'Keefe said, wiping a sleeve across his sweating forehead.

"You can sleep there until you get the house rebuilt," Remington ventured.

The farmer made no response. Remington looked for a nod or a reply or even a shifting of the man's eyes, but there was nothing.

"Your livestock and your chickens are still safe." He sat down on the edge of the trough, pulled out his bandanna, dipped it in the water, and slapped it on his head. A terrific wave of weariness almost made him fall over backward.

O'Keefe sat down next to him. Remington thought the man had aged a hundred years since the last time he had seen him. There was a great fatigue, a crushing burden, about him. O'Keefe's eyes looked toward the wreck that had once been a happy home, but they could not cry. He had used up all of the tears a man gets in one lifetime.

"How did it start, Elson?"

"The fire?" he asked absently. "I was out doin' some work behind the barn when I smelled the smoke. I come runnin' around here and the porch was already goin' pretty good by that time."

"You didn't see anybody?"

"Just the back of a fella ridin' away up that hill. The smoke was pretty thick by then, so I didn't get a real good look at him. I reckon he's the one that set it."

"He must have lit that kerosene lantern and tossed it up on the porch," Remington said.

"That's when I went in the house and started gatherin' up some of Sarah's stuff. I got a sack and a few dishes out of the kitchen. I guess the place went up faster than I thought it would. I was gonna come outside and try to put the fire out, but first I went into the bedroom. That's when you come in. I guess I wasn't thinkin' too clear, Marshal."

"Well, we got you out with your life. That's what counts."

O'Keefe made no reply, just grunted.

"At least you've got all summer to rebuild."

"Who done it? Who'd want to burn me out just for the damn spite of it? Who *was* that fella?"

"His name is Ramsey Clagg," Remington said, standing up. "He's the man I'm after. He's that killer I told you about."

"What's he got to do with me?"

Remington looked around. He didn't want to answer. Then

he saw his gelding, Shadow, stamping in a far corner of the corral.

"That's my horse, Elson! What's *he* doing here?"

"My hired man walked him in about an hour before the fire."

"The old Indian? Joseph Two-Shoes? He works for you?"

"Yeah. I have him do some odd jobs once in a while. How do you know him?"

"I traded my gelding and ten dollars to him to borrow his pony for a day or two. Where is he now? Maybe he saw for sure whether it was Clagg or not."

"I still don't know why he would've set that fire."

"Maybe he saw my horse in the corral and thought we were in the house together," Remington guessed. "But, knowing Clagg, I'd say he did it out of sheer meanness, trying to get me to ride after him."

"Ain't you after him anyway?"

Remington shook his head. He did not want to go into their encounter at Hell's Door and the brutal cat-and-mouse game that had been going on for the past few days.

"Elson, I've got to tell you something about Clagg."

"What? What is it?"

"Clagg's the same man who raped your wife."

"What? That bastard killed my Sarah? And he was just back here to burn my house down?"

"I'm sure it was him. He must have been trying to goad me into chasing after him so I'd fall into some kind of ambush."

The farmer stared up at him for a minute. "You knew, you knew the last time you were here, that the man you was trackin' was the same one killed my Sarah?"

"I was pretty sure."

"Why didn't you tell me? Why didn't you let me go with you?"

"The man's a killer. He murders people in cold blood as easy as you'd swat a fly. I've been after his kind before, Elson. I had to go alone. I couldn't take the responsibility of risking your life."

"By God, you ain't got no choice now, Marshal. I'm goin' with you whether you agree or not." He jumped to his feet.

The set of O'Keefe's lower lip told Remington that there was no use arguing with him.

"He killed your wife. Burned your house. I guess you got a right, Elson. But you go with me on one condition, and one condition only."

"What is it?"

"You won't kill him. I'm pledged to take him back to Stone County, Missouri, alive and in one piece. I'm an officer of the law, not a hired killer. Judge Barnstall didn't send me out to shoot the man like a mad dog—even though that's what he deserves. So you've got to swear to me—on your wife's grave—that you won't kill him. That you'll let me bring him in alive."

O'Keefe's left eye tightened. He clenched and unclenched his fists, trying to siphon off some of the anger. "All right," he finally said, through tight lips. "He's yours."

"It's understood, then. Saddle up, and if you've got a gun in the barn, bring it."

"I thought you just said—"

"I did. He's mine. But I want you to be able to defend yourself. If he starts shooting at us with that Sharps, I'll be damn lucky to cover myself, let alone you."

Remington went back and tended to the Indian pony while Elson O'Keefe was getting ready. The lawman already had told himself that it was a mistake to bring the farmer along, but after the tragedies that Clagg had caused him, there was no way he could deny him being in on the capture.

The marshal hoped it just stayed at that—a capture. He hoped O'Keefe would hold true to his promise.

The farmer came out of the barn leading a saddled gray mare. He carried his twelve-gauge shotgun but also had a long-range Henry rifle stuck into a boot on the horse.

"Where'd the old Navajo go?"

"I sent him off to a far corner of that field to clear some rocks," O'Keefe said, pointing. "I'm surprised he didn't see the smoke and come in."

"Maybe he's taking a nap," Remington said as they both mounted.

"Not old Joseph. He's honest. He's a little slow but he gives me a good day's work."

"You want to ride up that ways first?"

"We got time?"

"I don't think Clagg'll run too far. He wants to get to me as much as I want him."

They took off across the edge of the field, O'Keefe in the lead. Remington could tell from the way the man was sitting his horse that he was as tight as wet rawhide. The marshal wished now that he had lied. He wished that he had left O'Keefe behind.

When they got to the corner of the plot, it was evident that the old man had been working there. A few rocks had been rolled aside, but the Navajo was not there now.

Remington slid down from his horse to take a look at the ground. The dirt bore the slightest traces of moccasin tracks; then they led across some harder ground and Remington lost them.

"Probably just wandered off somewhere for a moment," O'Keefe said. "He'll be all right. C'mon, Marshal, let's get going."

"I'll take the point," the lawman stated.

"Huh?"

"Clagg knows me. He'll recognize my clothes, even from a distance. He doesn't want to kill me. If you're out in front, he'll knock you right out of the saddle."

"He knows you're a lawman and he doesn't want to kill you?"

"Remember what I told you about what he did to the deputy, Pete Trask?"

"Oh." O'Keefe's sun-reddened face went white for a moment.

"You stay a horse, maybe two or three horse-lengths behind me," Remington advised.

After riding back along the perimeter of the field, they found the trail that led out of the valley, the trail that Clagg had taken to escape.

Remington realized that he might be taking an unnecessary risk by putting O'Keefe at his back. If the man's thirst for revenge ran deep enough, O'Keefe might consider dropping the marshal to get to Clagg.

"Marshal!"

He reined the pony to a stop and looked around to O'Keefe. He half expected the man to be holding the shotgun on him to force him to dismount so he could continue the hunt alone.

Instead, O'Keefe was holding out his left hand. "I've got something here for you. Been keeping it in my pants pocket since the last time you left."

It was the marshal's silver badge.

Remington took it from the other's palm and pinned it back on his chest, where it belonged. The feeling of nakedness, of uncertainty, vanished. Even if he lost this fight against the big buffalo hunter, he would die a lawman, his badge a testimony to the way he had lived.

"Thanks, Elson. I appreciate it." Then, before he started up again, he said, "If you can get the Navajo to take care of your stock, you just might want to come with me, help me take Clagg and his buddies back to Missouri. I've got a feeling you might just want to be there when his sentence is carried out."

O'Keefe shook his hand, a strong, forceful grip. "Marshal Remington, you've got yourself a deal."

Now Remington was sure he would not be attacked from the rear. It had been a wise move. It gave O'Keefe a chance to focus his revenge on justice and not murder.

From this moment until he saw it happen, all the farmer would be able to think about would be a noose around Ramsey Clagg's neck.

Remington tried to guess what might be on the outlaw's mind, but it was no use. He was still convinced that Clagg intended some kind of trick that would either put the lawman on foot or surprise him enough to get the drop on him.

The way out of the valley was pocked with fresh hoofprints from Ramsey Clagg's horse. Remington was going to take as much satisfaction in this man's hanging as would Elson O'Keefe. The marshal had never before tracked an outlaw that had pushed him so close to the edge of his endurance.

Clagg was not only a dangerous man, he was as tough and

resourceful as they came. With a lesser sort, Remington would have been able to take him the day after they left Hell's Door. He was not sure how he was going to take Clagg alive, but he knew he had to try.

A faint groaning off to his left made Remington pull up. O'Keefe reacted more slowly, nearly crashing his horse into the back of the pinto.

Some trees clung to the side of the hill, and beside them a large clump of scraggly bushes. Remington swung down when he saw a pair of legs sticking out.

He ran over to find the old Indian, Joseph Two-Shoes.

The man's face was a bloody pulp. His right eye was already swollen almost shut. Dried blood caked his split lips. His withered hands were clasped across his abdomen, but they could not stem the flow of red that seeped between his fingers.

Remington knelt down. "Joseph? It's me. Marshal Remington. Can you hear me?"

The lips moved, though no sound came from them. O'Keefe appeared with a canteen, wet a bandanna, and patted it gently on the old man's mouth.

"He's been stabbed," Remington said.

"Good Lord. You got bandages in your saddlebag?"

"There might be some clean cloths in there. See what you can find. You just rest easy, Joseph. We'll try to help you." Remington told the Indian.

That trace of a smile flickered across the weathered face, an aura of sadness in it this time.

"Joseph Two-Shoes has . . . been wounded before," he whispered. He closed his eyes, then opened them.

Remington wanted to peel the Indian's hands back, but he did not want to let the flow of blood start full force again. O'Keefe handed the marshal the cloths. Remington slipped them to the edge of the old man's hands. Joseph felt them and worked them under, pressing the absorbent material against the wound.

"Big man," he said to Remington. "One you asked me about earlier."

"Don't try to talk."

"Does not matter. Hair, beard like fire."

"You were in the field?" O'Keefe asked.

"Walking in. Walking toward house. Saw fire."

"The big man rode out to you?"

A slight nod. "He asked if lawman in black clothes at farm. I say no. He get off horse, start hitting me. He ask where lawman's horse come from if you no here. I tell him I trade my pony for it. Then . . . he stab me."

O'Keefe closed his eyes very tightly. "Marshal, you get goin'. Go on! Get after him. I'll stay here and take care of Joseph."

Remington was about to stand up when a hoarse, wheezy breath coughed out of Joseph Two-Shoes' parched mouth. His hands fell away to the ground and his eyelids stopped their motion.

The lawman put his ear down and listened for the Indian's heartbeat. There was none.

Remington had been wrong. Elson O'Keefe was still able to summon up a few tears.

Chapter Fourteen

"That damn Clagg. That son-of-a-bitchin' Clagg."

"Yeah," Remington said flatly, agreeing with Elson O'Keefe's sentiments.

"Why would he want to go and murder an innocent old man like Joseph?"

"This man, this Clagg, he isn't like you and me, Elson. Either he can't tell the difference between right and wrong, or he just doesn't care."

The farmer stood up, ran a hand over his balding head, then slapped his hat back on. "One thing's for sure, Marshal. This Clagg has to pay for his crimes. There isn't a God in heaven if this man gets away scot-free."

"He's not going to get away," Remington assured him.

"I'd like to tend to old Joseph."

"You can if you want," the lawman replied, "but I've got to keep moving on. As cold as it sounds, there's nothing I can do for the Indian now. My responsibility is to catch up to Clagg."

O'Keefe stared down at the body. "You're right. It's crazy, but you're right. I have to leave him. I'll come back and bury him after we catch that bastard. Forgive me, Joseph."

They mounted up and set out on Clagg's trail. Remington realized now that the farmer could be a big help. O'Keefe was well acquainted with the country, every hill and valley, and he tried to foresee what the big man was doing.

"He's turning back east," Remington observed after a while.

"Probably try to go back out toward the plains," O'Keefe said. "It doesn't make sense. If Clagg wanted to bushwhack

147

us—and that's what *I'd* do if I was him—he should go west even farther into the mountains, where there's more chance to draw down on us."

Remington thought of the ambush *he* had made. He had been unsuccessful in clearing it from his mind.

"If I've learned one thing about Clagg, it's that he's unpredictable," the marshal said, with a snort. "When you get right down to it, the *only* thing predictable about the man is that he's *un*predictable."

"Sounds a lot like you. Unpredictable, I mean."

"Guess that's why this thing didn't end when it should have. Neither of us could really figure what the other was going to do."

"How long is it going to take us to put an end to it?"

"Not so long, I hope." Remington shifted in the uncomfortable saddle. He would not want to ride days on this makeshift seat. "You still planning to go back to Missouri with me?"

"Yeah. If I can get somebody to take care of my stock. I won't be able to get a good night's sleep until I see Clagg swing."

Remington knew the feeling. At first this had started as just another job, just another outlaw to be tracked down and brought back, but Ramsey Clagg's blatant disregard for morals and decency and everything that was right made Remington want to be one of the instruments that led to the man's extermination.

Throughout the day, Remington had to constantly rein the spirited pony back. It would serve no purpose to give him his head, to let him run. He would eventually tire if that happened, and then Clagg would have the upper hand again.

The marshal wished he could understand why Clagg was heading for open country. It was contrary to all common sense. They might even pass within a few miles of a fort, which could give Remington access to a troop of cavalry to help him. Remington realized that Clagg had him figured pretty well. The fugitive knew that this lawman enlisted no aid. He leaned on nobody else. He relied on his own wits and skill.

That was one reason Remington had let Elson O'Keefe

come along. It was entirely against his nature. It might be the trick that could take Clagg by surprise, if Remington could make good use of it.

O'Keefe's horse was big, well muscled. The mare loped along for hours with no sign of tiring. O'Keefe gradually edged ahead of his companion.

"Elson!" Remington finally shouted.

"Huh?"

"I want you to stay behind me."

"How come?"

"Clagg knows you. Killing you would be nothing to him, just like killing old Joseph. But he wants me alive; he's proved that a dozen times. You're an easy target out in front. Behind, you can use me for a shield."

"I don't like it," the man said, his face growing crimson.

"I know you're no coward," Remington replied. "But let's not get foolhardy, either. I didn't stay alive as a lawman for as long as I have by taking unnecessary chances."

"You're right," admitted O'Keefe, maneuvering the mare until he was a few horse-lengths behind Remington. "It's just that I'm so damn anxious to get the man. I can't wait for it to happen."

"We've got to be patient. Any hasty moves could mean the end of both of us. We'll get him, by and by."

"I just hope I can keep my finger off the trigger, Marshal."

"Remember the promise you made to me—on your wife's grave."

"You don't play fair, Marshal," O'Keefe said, something of a smile quickly crossing his face.

"Sometimes I can't."

They continued riding well into the afternoon, the farmer keeping up a jabbering monologue to cover his eagerness. Remington was just half listening to it, knowing that Clagg was far enough away that the talk would not cause them any trouble.

Over and over again the marshal tried to understand the killer's plan. He was about to give up on it when he realized that they had fallen into Clagg's trap.

They were in a valley of sorts, but it was nothing like the

choker canyon where Remington had staged his ambush. This place was more subtle, more inviting, but every bit as deadly.

The two riders were smack in the middle of it before Remington saw that it could be a trap. The hillsides were dotted with piñon and juniper. The lawman saw a dozen places where Clagg might be hiding. There was a half mile in back and a half mile ahead of them before they could get out of it.

"Marshal Remington?"

"I know. Just keep riding natural, Elson. Don't panic. Move your horse up. Try to get a little closer to me."

The first shot came screaming through, scorching the open space where Elson O'Keefe had been only a moment earlier.

The farmer froze, looking dumbly up the hill. Remington knew the next shot would find its mark unless he did something in a hurry.

First he tried to back his horse, forgetting that he was not on the well-trained gelding. The paint balked, rearing up and almost toppling over. It crashed into O'Keefe's mare, sending it in retreat.

Clagg fired again. The motion of the horses and the distance made them difficult targets. The second slug also missed.

Remington thought he saw a tiny puff of smoke from a clump of bushes, but he wasn't sure. He whipped out the Henry, balanced as best he could, and blasted in the direction of the cover. Unaccustomed to gunfire, his horse pranced around even more.

O'Keefe, panicked for something to do, pulled his shotgun out and got off one barrel. It made a tremendous noise, but the shot scattered ineffectively on the hillside twenty yards away.

"Save your ammo!" Remington shouted. "That thing's no good at this range."

Another shot boomed out from the hunter's Sharps. It was then Remington decided Clagg was trying to disable their horses but had been unable to do so because of the way they were dancing.

"There!" ordered the marshal. "Up toward those trees. We might be able to get some cover."

"Let's take him now," O'Keefe argued. "You go left, I'll go right. He can't contend with both of us. I'll keep him busy while you get the drop on him."

It was a stupid plan, born out of the desperation of a man pushed too far to see its flaws.

"C'mon, Elson. It won't work. Can't you see he's trying to get our horses? Let's get out of here before he drops one of them."

O'Keefe paid no attention. He started to gallop up the slope—exactly what Ramsey Clagg wanted him to do.

Another shot rang out, this one clipping off a quarter-inch chunk at the top of the mare's left ear. The horse whinnied and shook its head, pausing long enough for Remington to catch up with him.

"Listen to me, you damn fool! You're heading right into his gunsights. Get the hell out of here before you get killed."

O'Keefe reacted like a man waking from a deep sleep. Gradual comprehension came to his face. He looked up the hill. He looked back at the wildness in Remington's eyes.

"Jesus," the farmer muttered. He put his boots to the mare. It bounded away with remarkable speed. Remington got off a few more shots from the Henry, trying to provide cover fire. O'Keefe was already halfway up the opposite slope before Clagg risked another shot. It went wide of Remington's horse by five yards. The marshal shot twice more, then wheeled the paint and zigzagged him in retreat.

By the time Remington reached his friend's postion, the shots from Clagg had nearly stopped. The ones he did fire were only a testing, a harassment to further unnerve them. They were safely out of his range.

"I'm sorry," O'Keefe started to apologize as soon as Remington rode up.

"That's just the kind of thing I was afraid would happen," Remington said. His face was grim at the close brush they had both had with death. "Before we set out, I told you *I* would give the orders. I know you're anxious to get Clagg. I am too. But charging after him like that was a fool thing to do."

"I panicked. I was so damned scared I didn't know what else to do."

"Next time listen to me."

"If it wasn't for you, I'd be dead right now."

"We were lucky." Then Remington managed a grin. "Old Clagg must be a little shook up too. He's usually not that bad of a shot. Maybe he's getting tired."

"Just tired enough for us to take him."

"Tomorrow. This place is as good a one to camp as any. It'll be sundown soon. With two of us, we can stand watch. We're not going after him in the dark, and I don't think he'll come after us. It's a standoff, at least for now."

Night came and went without incident. Having another man with him, at least at this point, proved a definite advantage for Remington. Since he took half the watch, he could not sleep the entire night, but the sleep he did get was undisturbed and, for the most part, sound.

"So what's your plan?" O'Keefe asked him in the morning, when they were packing up their gear.

"Same idea you had yesterday—but a little more cautious," Remington said. "We'll split up and give him two targets to worry about. I'll try to get close enough to get the drop on him with my six-gun. Use the Henry, not the twelve-gauge, if you have to fire at something."

"Wouldn't it make more sense to take my shotgun if you're going in close? A man staring down those barrels usually has sense enough not to argue with you."

Remington scratched the back of his neck. "Maybe so, Elson, but the truth is, I've never used scatterguns much. Never had much faith in them as a gun you could swing around in a hurry. No, I'll stick with my Colt. I feel more comfortable with it."

"Well, this spot doesn't seem right for what you've got in mind. Too much open country. You'd be running from tree to tree, and you'd be exposed too much. I couldn't guarantee you cover fire all the time."

"Any spots up ahead that'd suit us?"

"Yeah, but remember, we're following him—or least we was last night."

"I'd bet he's already packed up and moved out."

"Hell, it ain't even dawn yet, Marshal."

"He's got a fox's head on his shoulders. He'll be figuring for us to hit him from two sides. It's the only logical plan of attack that could work."

"We could try to drop his horse," O'Keefe suggested.

"I thought of that. If we're chasing him, I don't reckon he'll let us get that close. When Clagg's men were chasing me, I held them back with my Henry, kept them out of range for trying that. Besides, a shot that long is risky. Might just as well hit the rider, and Clagg knows I know that."

"There is a spot up ahead, as we're coming down out of the foothills. It has a lot of scrubby trees and brush. Good cover. We might try it there, if Clagg heads for it. It's wide, so he'll likely pass through, but it means we'll have to catch up with him, overtake him."

"I think my horse is up to it," Remington said, patting the paint on the neck. "How about yours?"

"Old Sadie? You damn right she's up to it. You can ride Sadie all day, and she hardly works up a lather. Sorta like that gelding of yours we left back in the corral."

"Yeah, and I'm going back to pick him up as soon as we grab Clagg," answered the marshal as he swung up into the saddle.

"Remington, can I ask you a question?"

"Sure."

"Why'd you decide to go into this marshalin' business?"

"I've got no ties. No home to speak of," Ned Remington said, his voice suddenly sounding very tired. "One day, a lot of years ago, I got to wondering where I was going to end up, what was going to become of me. I wanted to count for more than just a pine-board grave marker that'd rot away five years after I was gone. I wanted to do something right. Wanted... this world to be a little better 'cause I'd passed through it. Sounds pretty corny, huh?"

"No," Elson O'Keefe answered, shaking his head. "Everybody needs somethin' to hang on to. Some's got religion, some's got other people. Guess you got the law."

"Yeah." A crooked grin formed on the marshal's face.

"The law doesn't keep you warm on a long winter night, or give you comfort when that hollow wind's blowing inside your heart, but when you're pulling in your last breath, you know you stood for something. You know you made a difference."

They rode off together in the darkness, moving cautiously toward the far end of the valley, where Remington dismounted, checked the ground, and, sure enough, found Clagg's tracks leaving the place. From what he could tell, they seemed fairly fresh. They had not started crumbling yet, and the dew that covered the rest of the ground was not on them.

"I'd say we're a half hour behind them. No more."

"We can make that up, easy. Do we push now?"

"Yeah. We want to catch up to them while he's still in that wooded stretch. That's where we'll make our move."

They rode hard, knowing even as the sun's first rays warmed the countryside that they were closing the gap between themselves and the big outlaw. Both men felt their hearts beat faster as they entered the thick area that O'Keefe had spoken of.

"You're right, Elson. This is a perfect place to make our move," Remington said, scanning the thickets of gambel oak and locusts.

Clagg came riding from behind some trees.

He was no more than a few yards away, reins clamped in his teeth, a Colt's pistol in each hand. He fired from left and right.

O'Keefe was between them, blocking Remington's shot. The marshal had not even pulled his sidearm when a bullet caught the farmer in the breastbone. Clagg disappeared back through the trees as quickly and unexpectedly as he had come.

Remington watched O'Keefe topple from his horse. The marshal debated whether to ride for Clagg. He jumped off the pony, using the mare as a shield, and ran over to his fallen friend. Remington knelt down, cradling O'Keefe's head in his hand. It was no good.

"Marshal. This is it for me. But you'll do it. You'll get Clagg for me, and Sarah, and Joseph. Promise me you will."

"I swear it, Elson."

"There. On my saddle. Take it. It's for Clagg. You know ...you know...

Elson O'Keefe went into a spasm of coughing, then was still. He had joined his Sarah.

Chapter Fifteen

Remington felt a lightness in his head, a dizziness he had never before experienced.

He could not believe O'Keefe had just died, a man he had been talking with, joking with, only a minute earlier. Remington had seen friends die before. During the war, some of them had even gone in his arms, like O'Keefe.

The marshal eased the dead man's head to the ground. Remington's immediate concern was that Clagg might still be around, that he might make another lightning attack or try to wound him from a distance with the Sharps.

It made sense, though, that Clagg would ride. He knew how enraged Remington would be at this death. Now it would be easy for the lawman to pull the trigger. Later, Remington would calm down and would remember his responsibility to the law.

Responsibility or not, Remington took the time to bury the farmer. He did not bury him as much as he piled small rocks on the body so that the animals could not get to it.

"You deserve better than this, Elson O'Keefe," Remington said as he lashed a makeshift cross together with a strip of rawhide. "You deserve to be up on that hill with your Sarah. Well, if the preachers are right, at least you're with her now in that better place."

The gray mare eyed the mound suspiciously, wondering where her rider had gone. Remington stared at her for a second. He could just imagine Shadow doing the same thing if O'Keefe had been putting *him* under instead. Despite the heat of the morning, it sent a cold shiver up the marshal's back.

Remington took off his hat. He had known some prayers once, many, many years ago, but he could not bring them back. All he could so was make a solemn promise that he would bring Ramsey Clagg to justice or die trying.

He could not waste time torturing himself because he had allowed O'Keefe to come along. That would cut his edge and would serve no purpose, anyway. It sure could not bring the farmer back.

"Sadie, old gal, you've got a new master now," Remington said as he found the stirrup and stuck his boot into it. The horse perked her ears up when she heard her name, even if it did come from an unfamiliar voice. The mare felt strong, powerful under Remington's thighs. She felt like an animal that could catch up with Ramsey Clagg. "C'mon, Horse," Remington whispered, taking up the reins of the skittish Indian pony. "You're coming too. I just might need a spare." He rigged a long enough line that the paint could trail a few lengths behind.

The gray was sturdy and larger than Remington had first thought. It was almost like riding a workhorse. The marshal would not have been surprised if O'Keefe had done some plowing with her. But she was saddle- and bit-trained and responded quickly to every command he tried. She was a horse to reckon with.

He the Henry in the boot, transferring the shotgun to the paint. After a few minutes of picking through the trees, he spotted Clagg's trail. As he followed it Remington's head swiveled from side to side watching for the slightest disturbance, the faintest indication that Clagg might still be in the area.

Late morning found Remington in more open country. The hills had become slopes, and trees were becoming more scarce. Firs and pines gave way to cypress and scrub oaks. Bunches of creosote bush huddled here and there. He skirted the edge of a prairie-dog town, watching he ground carefully so one of the horses did not step in a hole.

Pete Trask's map had only sketchy indications that the terrain ran from mountains to hills and plains. He knew he could

not be far from the Canadian River. He judged it to be somewhere north of him, but he did not know how far.

Despite the uneven ground, Remington was making good
time. The land was relatively level ahead. There was no sign
of Clagg on the horizon. Even the little spyglass could not
pick up the outlaw.

A coyote raced from a burrow only a dozen yards away,
spooking the little pinto. Remington calmed it with a few
quiet words and a gentle tug on the line.

He dug in his saddlebag and pulled out the last piece of
jerky. It was warm, salty. The more he chewed it, the tougher
it seemed to become.

Visions of a hot meal, a bath, and a hotel bed came to
mind. A wry grin formed on the lawman's face. He imagined
Ramsey Clagg was longing for the same sort of things, with
the exception of the bath, perhaps.

Clagg was moving fast. Remington liked that. It meant that
the big man had to be pushing his horse incredibly hard, and
what animal could hold up under that weight, over that distance, at that speed, for very long?

Remington had two horses. The gray was nowhere near
tiring, but if it did weaken, he could switch to the feisty paint,
turn him loose, and see just how fast he *could* run. Remington
was positive of it; he would overtake Ramsey Clagg before
sundown. By nightfall it would be over, one way or the other.

The marshal let the miles roll away behind him. The gray's
gait was firm, steady, a less graceful motion than that of Remington's gelding, but equally effective. Only when he noticed the pony tugging against the line, straining to keep up,
did Remington try to slow the big mare. A few times he dismounted, resting the animals for a few minutes while he
checked the trail. He estimated he was an hour, maybe two
behind, though it was hard to be certain.

When the Kiowas appeared over a rise, Remington was so
startled that he nearly fell off his horse.

It was just a small party of them, a dozen, maybe fifteen. It
might just as well have been a hundred. There was no way for
him to escape.

They had the uncanny ability to materialize like that,

seemingly out of nowhere. Remington had seen it before. He knew something about Indians, even spoke some of their language. He hoped he would get a chance to speak with this bunch.

None of them had made any threatening gestures. They had rifles, bows and arrows, but they kept them lowered. They were approaching him slowly, their horses at a walk. A couple of braves mumbled to each other. Remington could guess what they were saying.

A graying man, about fifty, apparently the chief of the band, rode out from the rest. The marshal noticed that the others kept their guns ready in case the white man tried anything foolish with their leader. The chief was a lean, impressive figure, sitting his horse ramrod-straight, reins in one hand and the other placed casually on his thigh. His hair trailed along and unadorned past his shoulders, and it was streaked with strands of white. He wore buckskin breeches and a threadbare cavalry jacket.

Remington kept eye contact with him. This was a situation that would call for all of his wits. His guns were worthless against the odds.

"You wear the sign of the law," the chief said, pointing to the badge.

"I am called Remington. I seek an evil man, a killer of women," he replied, in the native tongue.

The chief grunted. "Such a man deserves to die—slowly."

"I will see that he dies," Remington hoped that the Indian caught the implication that he wanted to be allowed to pass, to administer this justice.

"I am called White Crow." The Kiowa thumped his chest lightly with a closed fist.

"I have heard of you," Remington lied. "Your deeds are talked of around the night fires of my people. It is said you are a brave and honorable warrior." He voiced it loud enough that the others could hear. He hoped the chief did not see through it.

White Crow did not respond. Remington was not sure how to read the Indian's silence.

"I want to capture this evil man," the marshal continued.

"He rides east, like the wind. But..." The chief's eyes narrowed very slightly when Remington paused. He knew he had him. "I am losing time by trailing this second horse. Would the great White Crow accept this pony as a gift so that I may catch this killer of women?"

White Crow made a futile attempt to mask his emotion. Here was a horse for him, and all he had to do was let the white man through.

Remington realized they could kill him, take *both* his horses and all of his gear. But he had called the chief honorable. He had said that was well known in the camps of the white men. He was chasing a killer of women. And he had offered the pony as a gift.

The Indian smiled, showing yellowed teeth. Remington understood, without a word being spoken, that White Crow had seen through his farce.

"I take pony," he said. "And gun-that-shoots-many-times."

"No," Remington said, quietly but firmly. "I need that gun to slay the killer of women. The gun on the pony is more valuable anyway. It is the gun that shoots a hundred bullets with every shot. A hunter shooting birds or rabbits with this gun cannot miss."

"Good. I take pony and gun-that-shoots-many-bullets."

Remington wondered whether they could hear the sigh of relief he was letting escape between his teeth. He untied the long lead from the paint and handed it over to the Kiowa.

"What our people say of you is true. You are an honorable warrior. Peace to you and your people, mighty White Crow." Remington held up the open-palm salute. The Indian responded, and the marshal started to slowly walk the mare through the party. Without speaking, they backed their horses to let him pass.

Remington was an hour down the trail before the cold sweat quit flowing. He considered himself lucky that White Crow had appreciated a good bluff. If he had tried to ride through without giving the chief anything, it might have turned out differently.

He had no idealistic notions about Indians. It was true that they were fighting for their homeland, and, in their place, he would have done the very same thing. Their ways were not the white man's ways, and he guessed that, in a sense, the atrocities they committed were no worse than some of the things the white men had done to them.

In this instance, he had managed to slip through. He had used what he knew about them to force their hand. But if he had been rash or foolish, he had no doubt that these same "honorable" men would have given him a death far worse than anything Ramsey Clagg could concoct.

Remington consulted Pete Trask's map one more time. He was surprised to see—if he was correct in his bearings—that Clagg was headed directly toward Amarillo. And they were not that far from the Panhandle city. They would easily reach it before nightfall.

Why would this murderer ride to a city where he knew there was other law? Remington asked himself. Where a wanted poster had probably been circulated on him and people would know him on sight? Clagg had gone to Hell's Door to hide from civilized folk and the law; now he was going right to them.

Remington thought Clagg might be headed for Amarillo to try to break out Snuff Tully, but he quickly dismissed that idea. How would the outlaw have heard about Tully's capture? And besides, Ramsey Clagg owed allegiance to himself and himself only. He had used Virgil and Tully to commit the bank robbery, just as he had used the gang of bandits from Hell's Door to try to capture Remington. No, Tully was expendable. He was no longer a concern of the big man.

One possibility flickered through Remington's head, and as preposterous as it was, he had to admit it might be the truth. As the outlaws had been killed off or had deserted him, Clagg had lost his audience. He might be able to capture the lawman, even string him up and torture him, but the pleasure would not be as complete doing it alone. He had killed Pete Trask alone, but Trask had not taunted him, had not made a fool of him in front of the others.

Maybe that was it. Maybe Clagg wanted to humiliate him in Amarillo, in front of the entire town, in front of the law. To kill a chief territorial marshal right in the middle of town, then escape, unharmed, that was the scheme that turned in the mind of Ramsey Clagg. Word would get out all over the Nations. The telegraphs, maybe even the newspapers and penny dreadfuls, would pick it up.

That would appeal to Clagg. *That* would be worth taking these risks for.

Late-afternoon heat waves were still rippling off the ground when the lawman spotted Amarillo through his little telescope. There was scant life in the city on such a sweltering Texas day; most of the people were probably indoors or seeking the coolness of a shade tree.

As soon as Remington rode into town, he saw Ramsey Clagg's horse. Clagg had meant for him to see it, had left it tied outside a dilapidated saloon on the farthest outskirts of the city. Remington took it as a signal that the outlaw was inside, daring the marshal to an encounter.

His eyes on the saloon window, Remington rode up the street a ways before dismounting. Clagg's horse was in a sorry state. He had ridden it so hard that it was near collapse. It stood at the rail, shuddering from weakness, and every so often its knees would buckle and it would almost fall over. The animal would need weeks of rest before it could be ridden again.

Remington slid the long gun out of its sheath, then stepped into the shadowy refuge of a storefront porch. A fragile-looking man wearing a white shirt, brown pants, and a brown derby walked up. His hand trembled slightly as he extended it.

"I . . . s-see you're a U.S. marshal. Name's Wagner. I'm a whiskey drummer."

"Remington. Out of Stone County, Missouri."

"Missouri! Lord, that's a long ways away."

"Can I do something for you, Mr. Wagner?" Ned wondered.

"No. But I can do something for you. I was in that saloon there. The man you're after is still in there—with a trap laid for you."

"You want to tell me about it?"

"Yessir. I was in there, about a half hour ago, when this big redheaded, red-bearded fella comes bustin' in, swingin' that Sharps back and forth—"

"He have the buffalo gun with him, does he?"

"Yep. Anyhow, I was at the end of the bar . . . hell, that barman wouldn't know good whiskey if he tasted it. Well, like I was sayin', this big fella comes in, and damned if he didn't grab that bartender and tell him to give him a beer and make it cold if he valued his life."

"So he served one up?"

"Lordy, you think that big fella'd stop at one? He looked like he ain't had a beer in a month. He downed a half dozen of 'em, one right after the other."

Remington knew that it would take a lot more than six beers to make a man the size of Clagg drunk, but considering the heat, they wouldn't help him. Maybe he was still over there drinking.

"Then what happened?"

The drummer swiped a hand across his stubby beard. "The big fella pulled out one of them hoglegs, pointed it at the barkeep, and told him to hand over his sawed-off."

"Did he? How did Clagg know he even had one?"

"Guessed it, maybe. Most bartenders keep somethin' for protection. 'Cept this time it didn't do him much good."

"Then what?"

"Then the big fella goes behind the bar. He tells the bartender to get out from behind there and take a chair at one of the tables."

"So Clagg's behind the bar now?"

"He was when I left, just a couple minutes ago."

"How'd you manage to get out?"

"A fella fainted over in the corner, fell down, hit his head on a spittoon, made a hell of a racket. Clagg turned to see what happened and I slipped out the door."

"You tell the town law about this?"

"Not yet. I was just on my way there when I spotted you riding in."

"Do me a favor," Remington said.

"What's that, Marshal?"

"Give me about fifteen minutes before you tell the town sheriff. I want to take my crack at this man. I tracked him halfway across Hell."

The drummer looked at the marshal. He had a black growth of beard and dark circles under his eyes that showed he had not had a decent night's sleep for a long time. There was a rough edge to the man that made him look like a rattler just itching to strike.

"You got your fifteen minutes, Marshal."

"Thanks. Now, can you draw me a floor plan of that saloon?"

"Sure. Just let me tear a page out of my order book here." The liquor salesman ripped out a sheet of paper and began scratching on it with a pencil. Remington watched the drawing carefully as the man explained where the doors were, where various people were standing and seated, and the field of view that Clagg had.

"Much obliged, Wagner. That's what I needed to know."

"When does your fifteen minutes start?" the drummer asked.

"Right now."

The man nodded and pulled out a tarnished pocket watch. Remington walked across the street, figuring that Clagg would not be able to see him out of the front saloon windows at this angle.

When the marshal saw the hardware store, a plan sprang into his mind.

Five minutes later, Remington was crawling under the windows of the building, trying to get a look at Clagg. It was no use. He could not see the outlaw without being seen himself. He would just have to rely on the drummer's drawing and hope that Clagg had not moved.

Behind the hardware store was a wooden ladder that Remington had borrowed. He ran down the dusty alley with it, hoping no one would shout at him, hoping there would be no noise to give him away.

It was just tall enough. He leaned it against an attached shed at the rear of the building, climbed to the tar-papered roof of the lean-to, then scrambled to the shingles of the saloon.

Remington took short, cautious steps. The gritty roof was hot under the soles of his boots. He could hear the raspy voice of Clagg drifting up from the open windows. It was mostly bragging, senseless bravado about what he was going to do if Remington ever showed his face.

The marshal crawled over to the rusty stovepipe protruding from the roof. This was going to take some doing, some perfect timing.

The pipe had a conical cap on it. When Remington pried it off, it gave a grating squeak. He paused, listening. There was no break in the big man's monologue.

From his back pocket, Remington extracted the stick of dynamite he had bought at the hardware store. He trimmed the fuse with his throwing knife until it was only a few inches long.

First he checked the roof behind him. It had a galvanized gutter, angling directly above the side window.

He knew the potbellied stove was in a back corner of the saloon. From Wagner's drawing, he knew that no one was near it. The rest he would leave to chance.

Remington popped a sulphur match, lit the explosive, and dropped it down the metal chimney.

The roar from the dynamite sounded like a dozen cannons going off at once.

When the concussion boomed out of the top of the stovepipe, a geyser of black flakes spewed into the air. Remington was already on the edge of the roof, in position. He knew he did not have much time.

He gripped the metal gutter with both hands. Pushing off with his legs, he swung out, then back.

Remington crashed through the side window and into the center of the saloon's main room.

The potbellied stove and its ascending stovepipe, both caked with soot from the previous winter's use, had blown apart in a choking cloud of blackness. The soot still hung in the air, obscuring everyone's vision.

Ramsey Clagg stood behind the bar, a big Colt in each fist,

hammering out bullets helter-skelter, trying futilely to hit the man he knew had done this.

Remington slipped in low, beneath the deadly gunfire. He knew that with his black clothes, the cloud in the air, and the soot in Clagg's eyes, the big man could not see him. The marshal was tempted to draw his own pistol, but he did not trust himself to keep from pulling the trigger.

Instead, he swiped a wooden chair off the floor and smashed it across the buffalo hunter's skull. Clagg wavered, but he did not go down. His left-hand gun clattered to the floor. Remington snatched one of the chair legs from the bar and used it to swat the redhead's other revolver out of his hand.

But Clagg reached out, groping, and caught the front of Remington's shirt. The marshal set his boots on the rail and threw his body backward.

Clagg's grip was so tight that he was yanked out on top of the bar. Remington slammed his fists into the sides of the killer's head. Clagg let go with his left hand long enough to swing it down in a stunning roundhouse blow. His fist went high of Remington's chin, though, and bounced off the marshal's forehead.

Remington stuck his hands into Clagg's mop of red hair and rammed the giant's head down on the bar. The right-hand grip loosened. Grabbing Clagg's shirtfront, Remington pummeled the man's face with a series of short punches.

The soot was still too thick in the air for the marshal to see that his opponent's eyes had glazed over. Ramsey Clagg flailed his arms in a final useless defense.

Remington jerked him out over the bar and let him crash to the floor in a pool of blood and beer.

"Clagg, I can't even remember all the charges against you," the marshal said, swaying slightly, "but you're going back to Missouri, to stand trail for every last one of them."

The big freight train chugged in, smoke and cinders puffing from the locomotive's conical stack. Remington had relished the hours of sleep the train ride had allowed him, and it had made sense to transport the three prisoners this way.

There would have been too much ground to cover on horseback, guarding three murderous outlaws. Now, as the train pulled into Stone County, the marshal recalled all the hard riding and quick thinking that had brought him out of this alive and put these three men in chains.

Jake Virgil stepped out of the end of the passenger car first, holding his manacled hands in front of him. He had leg irons on, as did Snuff Tully, who followed him. Ramsey Clagg stumbled out next, his face bruised and swollen. But they were alive, dammit. Remington had brought the sons of bitches back alive.

They made the ride back to the Stone County courthouse in silence. A deputy drove the team while Remington guarded the three sullen men sitting in the bed of the wagon.

After they secured the prisoners in the cells below the building, Remington went to Judge Barnstall's chambers. Barnstall was taking a recess between cases. Remington rapped on the door three times.

"Judge Barnstall. It's Ned Remington."

"Come in, come in, Remington. It's good to see you again," Barnstall said, offering him a glass of bourbon. "You get your men?"

"They're in the jail right now," Remington answered. "And you can tell the prosecutor to add three murder charges to Clagg's docket. Farmer out west of the Texas Panhandle, name of Elson O'Keefe, his wife Sarah, and their hired man, a Navajo named Joseph Two-Shoes."

Barnstall scribbled the names on a piece of stationery.

Remington reached in his saddlebag. "Before he died, O'Keefe gave me this. Said it was for Clagg. I think you'll know what to do with it."

Remington tossed the object on Barnstall's desk.

It was a heavy coil of rope.

CHANCE

The Maverick with the Winning Hand

A blazing new series of Western excitement featuring a high-rolling rogue with a thirst for action!

by Clay Tanner

CHANCE 75160-7/$2.50US/$3.50Can
Introducing Chance—a cool-headed, hot-blooded winner—who knows what he wants and how to get it!

CHANCE #2 75161-5/$2.50US/$3.50Can
Riverboat Rampage—From ghostly spirits on the river to a Cajun beauty who's ready and willing to stoke up big trouble, Chance is the man women love and varmints love to hate!

CHANCE #3 75162-3/$2.50US/$3.50Can
Dead Man's Hand—Framed for murder, the gambling man breaks out of jail and in a fast shuffle heads upriver to settle the score.

CHANCE #4 75163-1/$2.50US/$3.50Can
Gambler's Revenge—His riverboat stolen—all nice and legal—Chance had to look for justice outside the courtroom...if he wanted the *Wild Card* back!

KILLSQUAD

by Frank Garrett

WANTED: A world strike force—the last hope of the free world—the ultimate solution to global terrorism!

THE WEAPON: Six desperate and deadly inmates from Death Row led by the invincible Hangman...

THE MISSION: To brutally destroy the terrorist spectre wherever and whenever it may appear...

KILLSQUAD #1 Counter Attack   75151-8/$2.50 US/$2.95 Can
America's most lethal killing machine unleashes its master plan to subdue the terrorquake planned by a maniacal extremist.

#2 Mission Revenge   75152-6/$2.50 US/$2.95 Can
A mad zealot and his army of drug-crazed acolytes are on the march against America...until they face the Killsquad.

#3 Lethal Assault   75153-4/$2.50 US/$3.50 Can
The Fourth Reich is rising again, until the Hangman rounds up his Death Row soldiers for some hard-nosed Nazi-hunting.

#4 The Judas Soldiers   75154-2/$2.50 US/$3.50 Can
A madman seeks to bring America to its knees with mass doses of viral horror, but Killsquad shows up with its own bloody cure.

#5 Blood Beach   75155-0/$2.50 US/$3.50 Can
The Hangman and his Killer crew go halfway around the world to snuff out a Soviet/Cuban alliance seizing control in Africa.